WHEN

THE JOURNAL NON/FICTION PRIZE

When

Stories

Katherine Zlabek

MAD CREEK BOOKS, AN IMPRINT OF
THE OHIO STATE UNIVERSITY PRESS
COLUMBUS

Mad Creek Books, an imprint of The Ohio State University Press.

Library of Congress Cataloging-in-Publication Data

Names: Zlabek, Katherine, author.

Title: When : stories / Katherine Zlabek.

Description: Columbus : Mad Creek Books, an imprint of The Ohio State University Press, [2019] | Winner of the 2018 The Ohio State University Press "The Journal" Non/Fiction Prize

Identifiers: LCCN 2019012042 | ISBN 9780814255469 (pbk. : alk. paper) | ISBN 0814255469 (pbk. : alk. paper)

Subjects: LCSH: Middle West—Fiction. | Short stories, American.

Classification: LCC PS3626.L33 A6 2019 | DDC 813/.6—dc23

LC record available at https://lccn.loc.gov/2019012042

Cover design by Regina Starace
Text design by Juliet Williams
Type set in Adobe Garamond Pro

Contents

HIGGINS 1

HUNTING THE RUT 21

LOVE ME, AND THE WORLD IS MINE 35

IF THERE IS NEED OF BLESSINGS 51

SO VERY NICE 69

FENNIMORE 85

PASSING 101

LET THE RIVERS CLAP THEIR HANDS 117

CIRCUMSTANCES 129

ACKNOWLEDGMENTS 143

Higgins

My aunt pushed in the tape and said, "Don't you want to see your father on the stage?" She was putting on a parody of my grandmother, her mother. She hunched and rubbed her hip. She smoked a fake cigarette. "He stole the show, of course. No one could play the role like your father."

The role was Henry Higgins. Professor Higgins. My father had been in a high school production of *My Fair Lady,* and my grandmother could not get over it. The previous Christmas, she'd had copies made for any family member in possession of a VCR. My grandmother's pride was vulnerable to mockery. My father was at this time forty and successful in insurance. I was fourteen, and about to start waitressing at Cal's, a burger joint where I would wear a hip belt with a coin dispenser. A strangely sexual touch at an otherwise wholesome establishment. My aunt, who was unmarried, was sure the waitressing would not go well. Aunt Kay was a humanities professor in Madison. I did not know what that meant at the time, to profess the humanities. As a whole, the family felt a better attitude would have gone a long way with her. Her lips were always some bright color, flagging the world's attention. I believed every word she said.

The tape rolled, but this was no high school production. It was Hepburn and Harrison and flowers, flowers. "Hmph," my aunt said, "must have been mismarked." But we didn't stop. There was no need. It was my father all over: the pointing, the tone, the commands. *No strawberry tarts for you, Eliza. Wear this necklace. Stand here and choke for all I care.*

I stayed with my aunt for a week. It was something done then. As though summers required some mix-up, some change of pace. She lived only an hour away. Others went to the Bahamas or took a pottery class at the vo-tech. This was my last summer as a child, the last summer I would need to be entertained in that childish way. During the week, she started calling me Eliza. She bellowed it down the stairs or across the café—bellowing came naturally to her, due to her profession. My real name was Lottie, and I avoided using it whenever I could. It's unclear what a parent is preparing the child for when she's named Lottie.

*

Four years later, when I graduated valedictorian, my father held a picnic in the backyard. There were lawn games and ham sandwiches put together by the grocer. The standard marble sheet cake I've since learned to despise. Aunt Kay sat on a massive plastic tub in which we kept a volleyball net and foldout chairs. She wore a thick black skirt that spread out like a blanket underneath her, and she ate her food in small, slow bites. My father stood at the grill, turning bratwursts and pointing with the tongs to people he thought would amuse her.

"Not bad, our Lottie?" He was talking about me. About the job he'd done, making me.

"No, not bad," my aunt said. "But you'll have to get a dog. Who else will do your tricks once she's gone?"

I had been on a streak, shooting free throws. A crowd had gathered around me and was cheering. I don't believe anyone else heard what my aunt had said. When someone fed me the ball, I didn't know whether or not to shoot. I'd never liked basketball, and I realized I would never again see any of the people circled around me once the summer was finished. I'd spent the last several years of life excelling in unnecessary skills that I'd not desired. Throughout high school the faculty had been desperate for field trips, and it seemed we took an early bus to the UW—my future alma mater—once a month, if not once a week, to watch Mexican hat dancing, the opera, the Capitol Christmas tree being lit. Or to attend some specialty camp for peer-building or pitching softball. It was an education that left me uncertain of what philosophy was, but confident I could order churros in the language of origin.

That was when Sadie came. She whipped around the garage with her arms spread wide, her bangs curled and sprayed like a beach wave, saying something stupid and sociable—Oh! or Ah!—and then she tripped on the edge of the concrete and bloodied her mouth. The slow reflexes of the rich. As far as I know, she left her tooth chipped that way for the rest of her life. It was the style, for a time.

"Rough stuff," my aunt had said and laughed. That was the first real laugh I'd heard from her. Two years would pass before I could begin to understand that laugh.

*

Sadie lived one town over. Same age. She started working at Cal's the summer I did, before high school. A little before or a little after—I can't remember. Seniority was not an issue with her. She was the kind of person who always needed telling what to do, cleaning up after. There were three waitresses who worked the night shift. Summer nights were best for tips because of the baseball leagues, the slow-pitch beer teams. Straw wrappers blown across the tables, a line out the door. Cal's was famous for its root beer and cheese curds. There was a drive-in, too. Thirty years before, the waitresses roller-skated to the cars, but that was all done by the time I got there. Insurance reasons, I'm sure, or so my father said. Even on a busy night, with the drive-in speakers shaking out order numbers and oldies, you could hear the crickets creaking along the hayfields.

At fourteen, I was no talker. I got in and got out, was pleasant enough, and must have smiled. This is why I got so many big tips or dimes arranged into a heart or napkins with numbers and short proclamations of love written on them: they did not know me well.

Sadie talked. She stood there with a pot of coffee and chatted as though she'd had just the one table over for a dinner party. The manager insisted Sadie keep her long hair, frizzed and eager, in a ponytail, but still it wrapped over her shoulder and bushed out over her nametag and curled over fries. She rarely wrote down an order, and so she'd rush back to the table, laughing, saying, "What was that you wanted again? A double—no, a triple? Milkshake?" So easy with them. Because she talked so much, she was never tipped well. No one in Wisconsin wanted to tip someone so confident, who had just learned so much about you. Also, Sadie's father was famously rich.

Nowadays, there would be a stew about a girl like her taking a job like that, but this was before the recession. Jobs in Wisconsin were easy to get and were taken for the experience and to keep busy. The money was a side effect, or so it seemed then. Or so it seemed to girls like us. (I can say "us" now, about those teenage girls we were. I can see that we were not so different as I then thought. It was the wedge of feeling different from someone that changed me. There is no us now. *Isn't that sad?* Sadie asked, years later at some wedding. Or, no, it wasn't rhetorical. She said, *Do you think that's sad?*) There was not so much for a teenager to buy before the age of computers and cell phones: movie tickets and eye shadow. A cassette tape. My father had me cover all of this and part of our family's groceries and my share of the phone bill. But by the time high school started, I spent nearly nothing. I went where Sadie went, vice versa, too, and her father paid the way. "An investment, like anything else," my aunt later said. "Kept her busy. Can you imagine the stir if that girl had gotten pregnant?"

Pregnancy had been scheduled out. Her father picked her up from her night shifts, and he dropped her off at four, too. That was how I first met him, a month into our jobs. Sadie and I had finished mopping the floors, and the third waitress—also the night manager—had taken our money belts and counted our bills and coins. The freshly mopped floors smelled like old grease and urinal cakes and I hated to realize at the calm end of every shift that I smelled the same way. I would wonder how I dared to smile like a pretty girl, smelling that way. Sadie was always some dollars off, and the manager took it out of what tips she had—a routine that no longer frustrated the manager when she saw how easily Sadie parted with the money. In fact, I'd become certain that the manager was skimming Sadie's tips because she was Sadie. It mattered so little I didn't say a thing. It actually pleased me, and it would have been better only if Sadie could recognize an insult.

The night I met Sadie's father, Sadie left work twirling her apron in the air like a lasso, and her nametag and order pad went flying into the darkness. I liked to park in the back, in the dark, because I didn't have my driver's license yet. My father suggested this routine and thought it taught me something. It was eleven. A black Lincoln Navigator was idling across the street with its lights off, and women everywhere know this means danger. Or I thought, stupidly, the police had found me out for driving illegally.

I was quick to find her things. When I handed them to her, she was still laughing that she'd flung them. She laughed like Santa Claus—*Ohhoho*—and bent over her knees. I was always sure this laugh could not be genuine, and so it was hard to laugh with her unless I had the energy to fake it. "Come and meet my dad," she said when she caught her breath. She took my hand and led me to the Lincoln. This was no relief for me. I did not act silly or slow—act young—in front of parents. Especially with high school just weeks away. It seemed then like the pinnacle of maturity, that we'd all be given a studded leather jacket and cigarettes upon entrance.

"You must be Lottie," her father said, and held out his hand. "Mike."

Nothing about the scene was familiar or common in this town. He wore a dress shirt and tie. He had a car phone cupped in his lap on top of a pad of legal paper, the phone cord curled into a cup of steaming coffee. He had paused a conversation to shake my hand. My mother had told me calls on car phones cost ten dollars a minute.

Then Sadie said many things quickly. Acted out little stories about who she had run into, *run into,* not waited on. All the hilarious—there is no other word to match her tone—things I'd missed, that I'd not known I participated in while refilling sodas and switching out ketchups. Was this how others spoke to parents? I'd thought

I was supposed to spell out drudgery—let them know I'd earned my keep for another night. He nodded and wrote notes on his pad as she spoke—"Good business practice," he'd later say. "Keep tabs on everyone." The person on the phone kept waiting. Sadie had Mike's eyes, and though I'd never noticed them on her before, they were big discs, just one shade of blue away from seeming blind.

When he asked if I needed a ride home, I told him I had one and pointed back into the dark. I did not feel this was lying.

"You're only Sadie's age."

"My father has an arrangement," I said.

"We'll take you tonight. Just this once."

And so, I sat stinking of fast food in his leather backseat while Sadie fiddled with the radio station, looking for the perfect song. "It's a special moment," she insisted—"We've got you now!" And then the laugh. Mike cut his phone call short. He knew where I lived—fifteen minutes out of his way, a town away from Cal's and in the country. Sadie said, "It's practically his job to know where people live. He spends his life in the car, on the phone." I could see her eyes glow back at me in the dashboard light. I was not sure how someone could become rich talking on a car phone—or tan or muscled—but he was all of these things. "We'll be here at 3:30 tomorrow," he said when he pulled up, and they were only five minutes late. That was the way it went until we got our licenses. My father was furious with me for his having to make a special trip to bring the car back from Cal's, until he heard it was Mike. "How'd you manage that?" he asked.

*

I had thought high school would be different from what it was. "It should have been," is what my aunt would later say, "but you know how he gets." I should have known whether she meant my father or Mike. I didn't. I had imagined sweet dates and long baths, dreaminess and lies. But there was no time. My father required a sport, and so I played basketball. To help, Mike took Sadie and me to camps, special practices, leagues. The men along the bleachers shook his hand, loosened ties. He talked strategy in the Lincoln. Sadie had a habit of eating corn chips slowly and nodding and asking questions, all while drifting to sleep. There were clubs that Mike and Sadie told me I should join—over a dozen. I was the president of the Future Business Leaders of America. At the right kind of party, I will share this as a joke.

Sadie called so often that my mother, who rarely said anything at all, began to lie about my being there. She was sure Sadie was in love with me. "What do you do over there all the time?" she asked.

"We talk. Mike takes us to restaurants," I said. "I ate calamari last night."

"Oh, God," my mother said. "I'm surprised you're not dead." My mother believed all food that was not canned or frozen was lethal.

*

Aunt Kay planned a party for the night I moved in with her. I was twenty, and this was the start of my third year at university in Madison. This was not a party for me—she would never be so crass, and she certainly didn't call it a party. That afternoon, she had stood at my bedroom door and said I was *welcome,* with a gesture of the arm that seemed to indicate exhaustion. A thick black belt pinched her waist in such a way that it seemed any sudden strike would snap her in two. A clean break. She needed to stop at the caterer's to chat with the sommelier, buy flowers. Without intending to, she was already teaching me the delicacies of her world. She wore heels in the house, and I heard her walk down the hall and up the stairs and right out the front door. To this day, I have never known a person better able to leave quickly.

At the party, a man mixed a drink for me and asked, "What kind of music do you like?" He poured one long measure of gin into a tumbler.

"Everything," I said, which was not the right answer. "I was in a musical once." A lie. The man taught philosophy. His distaste was visible and rote, though he was only twenty-five or thirty, as far as I could tell. His hair stood on end in the saddest way, with a slight wave and a center part. "I played Eliza Doolittle," I said. "I made Diane the hairdresser cry."

My aunt overheard but said nothing. She was fussing with Brie rind and a knife smeared with marmalade. It was clear she did not want to get her hands dirty. "This cheese has gotten out of hand," she said to some man who was watching her. She laughed. He stepped toward her and became cozy and helped her. That laugh had worked after all. The grand performance of a single woman. But a moment later, the man was at the elbow of some skirt with a French accent. It wasn't enough. It would never be enough for these people. *Intellectuals,* that's what I learned to call them that year.

Aunt Kay's house was massive—two stories and the finished basement I lived in. One end of the living room had wide windows the height of the ceiling that looked out over Lake Mendota. Her guests hovered there, all forty or fifty of them, mostly artists and faculty. Night had fallen, and the yacht lights shone across the waves. Some jam band tested its equipment at the university union across the way. They had one final show before the semester began and changed everything. Sadie would return the next day from a mother-daughter vacation in Cancun, and she'd promised to stop by with a souvenir. I had not yet unpacked my boxes.

I touched the young professor on the elbow—it was the gin—and meant to excuse myself, but when I turned to leave, Mike stood in the doorway. An adolescent panic shot through me—that I had missed a shift at Cal's, or Model UN. He wore khakis and his shirt was buttoned to the collar. His blonde hair was parted and slicked. He stood there and scanned the room with his hand on his beeper. I assumed he'd come for me—Mike had met me in private before and asked that I persuade Sadie to take a particular class, avoid specific parties, abandon the boys he deemed beneath her. Poor Mike, I'd thought, finding himself in this crowd. But he walked past me and took my aunt by the waist. She startled, curved into him and kissed him. She wiped her lipstick from his mouth with her thumb and undid his top two shirt buttons. "Give me these, at the very least. What a stick in the mud, Michael."

I have not mentioned Sadie's mother until now. Perhaps she seemed unimportant. But of course the wife of a man like Mike is important—not to mention well-kept and healthy. She was a seamstress before she married Mike. Second-generation Greek, and he'd met her while she worked at the family alteration business. She still clipped coupons for frozen pizzas and kept a little sewing room in their basement, where I had watched her fix my hems many times. She ate homemade baklava while she sewed and taught Sadie and me about stitches and the importance of college while she worked. Sadie was nothing like her. I believe having married Mike—*Michael*—was a shock from which Sadie's mother never recovered, and I often thought of her and wished her joy. There was not, it seemed, much joy in her.

"The king has come," the French woman said when she saw Mike. "Let us good peasants bow."

She meant for Mike to hear, of course: I know now that the money is never welcome at the party. The party will always be bitter for relying on the money. Someone snickered. The man next to her said, "Come now, Inès," and the party continued as though my world had not been shaken.

"I see you two have met," Mike said to me. He shook hands with the philosopher. Ryan, he called him. Whatever discomfort Mike experienced at my discovery hardly registered. He kept his hand at my aunt's back. With this small gesture, I knew he would deny nothing about the affair. Later, I realized he must have planned it this way, wanted me to find them out in a crowd that took the two of them for granted. In that moment, I realized Aunt Kay was shorter than I was by an inch at least, and that was with her heels on. She said to Mike, "You're absolutely right. I can't believe I didn't think of the match before."

Mike had given me away as though I were his daughter. Ryan and I began dating. He was a graduate assistant, not a philosophy professor. A poseur. Good-looking, after a haircut. More importantly, he was Mike's nephew. Years later, Ryan would say, "I don't know what happened. I talked to Mike at that party—he pulled me aside, we had a drink—he gave me his blessing. 'It's okay, go ahead, it would make sense . . .' It felt like an occasion." We had been discussing why we'd gotten married in the first place. We were only two years in.

After that party, my life's cast jumbled their costumes, embraced brief and startling expansions of character. First, there were simple dates. Indian food, an art house production, a Saturday football game for which Ryan dressed in red. There was the rare double date with Mike and Aunt Kay in some restaurant so expensive I could only imagine what my father would say. Most often, Mike would have Aunt Kay buy the simple luxuries—tins of caviar, prime rib, stuffed olives, Winnimere wrapped in spruce, kumquats. Only the liquor store sold these things. The four of us would sit at Aunt Kay's house drinking tempranillo, social for an hour or two before we would go in pairs to our separate floors and rooms. An education, that's what a certain set calls this. I did not see Sadie except for rushed coffee and bagels once a week before a biology lab, which I was failing. I did not take the failing seriously. Mike could get me a job in Chicago—either he had said this, or I assumed it. Chicago was the only place to go, it seemed, if you didn't want to stay in Madison.

*

I drove home that first day of Christmas break. It was habit. I picked up shifts at Cal's, and during slow hours painted evergreen garlands hung with stockings along the wide windowpanes. The floors were sloppy with snow carried in by boot lugs, and I kept busy with a dry mop as livestock drivers came in groups to discuss beef and pork prices after auction. Twice, Sadie came to Cal's and sat in my section. She ordered elaborate meals that she fidgeted with while waiting for me. The burger sitting in its wrapper, the batter pulled from onion rings, a puddle of milkshake. I did not understand how an adult could spill a milkshake without noticing, and I wondered whether my thinking this was an initial sign of maturity or of ugliness. The bounty, the anxious waste—all typical of Sadie. I don't know if I began to pity her because she knew nothing of her father's affair, or because her loneliness was then so obvious.

One night, in that long week between Christmas and New Year's, the two of us went to a club in Fennimore. Sadie had insisted that we do it the right way. She meant the way we'd done it once or twice before, and so we pulled my car over along the side of a gravel road and changed out of the sweaters our families had seen and into tube tops. Snow fell on the windshield and melted into streams. Sadie had brought a mixtape of rap songs she'd lifted from the radio. It clicked to the end and whirred, rewinding. Working under the dome light, Sadie pressed a dark glitter onto my eyelids and lined her lips with a violet that looked black in the night. Twice, we were caught in passing headlights, and she shook as though taken by a chill. She let out a soft, high "Ah" as she tensed her bare shoulders, coy, I suppose, in the sense of being deliciously exposed, rebelling, warm and alive in the grip of dim winter.

At the bar, Sadie ordered several shots of vodka. We danced on a stage along with the high school students who had sneaked from the cornfield and in through the back doors, which were open for the cold air. We sweated. Sadie held my face between her palms and yelled through the music. She said that Ryan had stolen me from her. Her own cousin! Then she laughed her strange, bent-over laugh and some redheaded man took her from behind and began to dance with her.

A boy spun me out and I did not spin back into him. I walked to the bar for water and wondered whether I was expected to call Ryan. He could be ashamed of me or, as he sometimes was, eager that I cultivate core memories. Touchstones, he called them. The glitter Sadie had shadowed my eyes with began to scratch, and I could not stop blinking against the sparkling lights. I went to the bathroom and dabbed at my eyelids with a paper towel off in a corner while chatting with a woman who sat in the sink and pulled off her pantyhose. Once the woman left, I stood in front of the mirror with smudged, bloodshot eyes and regretted leaving my aunt behind in Madison over break, but particularly that night. She and I did not often get drunk with Mike, though he was the one who poured, who ordered another. Waited, as if he wanted more from us. I thought some evenings of Sadie's laugh, her whole exaggerated self, and understood it had grown from this sense of expectation. I caught myself setting up stories in the grand manner. A big rolling of the arms, a gesture with my glass. Mike had been in his home when I picked up Sadie earlier that evening, talking on his phone and writing notes between the advertisements in *The New York Times* while he paced beside the kitchen countertop. He had glanced up and waved as we left, cool and fatherly as when we were still two girls on our way to a late-night dribbling practice, up to nothing but making him proud. I did not care for the situation. I imagined Aunt Kay alone in Madison, grading papers out of spite, as she sometimes did, writing harsh things on the assignments of business majors, students studying finance or marketing. Soulless, she called them. She did not believe in journaling or crying or television, and kept no companions. Ryan often warned me of defaulting toward these same traits.

There was vomiting in the toilet behind me. I bent to wash my face. The drain was rusted over and slow. I watched the green rings around it dance. A lipstick had been dropped, and there were oily red slashes across the basin. I did not stop scrubbing until I heard someone calling my name. It was the red-haired man who had pulled Sadie away. He had broad, furred knuckles, and he gave me two paper towels before producing Sadie from the bathroom stall, where she was leaning and straining the joints that held it together. "Oh-ho!" she said when I stepped aside and she saw herself in the mirror. She smiled as though she had told a joke, and the man bent to slap one of those paws across his thigh. There were tears in her eyes from the vomiting and her chest was blotched with red. The man's name was Tom. It was only 10:30.

*

They were dating, had been dating. Tom and I stood outside in the gravel parking area while Sadie sat on the passenger seat in his truck. She sat facing out to us, with the door open and his fleece-collared denim jacket over her shoulders. Her bare feet dangled over the running board. Heat and soft twanging music were slowly swelling out from the truck cab. There were low-hanging snow clouds, and against them I saw the exhaust billow behind Tom and up into the night. Tom reached into the glove box and offered me a stocking cap. We'd left our jackets in the car. I took the cap and picked the alfalfa from its weave while we discussed what to do next.

Sadie did not have her apartment keys. Our families were best avoided. Tom lived on the family farm he was set to inherit and had renovated a portion of the hayloft as a sort of makeshift apartment, to signify his autonomy. It was not fit, he insisted, for ladies. I imagined cobwebs and a straw-dusted wood floor, sooty girlie posters hung with tape over the squares of milk pane glass. "The toilet, for starters," he said, and meant to continue before I agreed that we should go back to Aunt Kay's, where there was an unused bed and bath beside mine on the bottom floor. It was, of course, Mike's house. My aunt could not have afforded to live in a house like that. On nights when Mike had upset her, she called it the compound. Take me back to the compound, she would say whenever she felt he had rushed an evening out for the sake of his business. That was what Mike did: business. I know no more about it.

Tom drove us up to Madison in his red Tacoma pickup. We drove with the windows down, for the fresh air's sobering effects. In the side mirror, I watched the rust fly from the wheel wells each time we hit a pothole along the highway. It was a half-hour drive, and Sadie became sick twice. She sat on the seat between us, and I gave her Tom's stocking cap to vomit into. It was a favorite cap, navy blue, and there was much deliberation regarding what to do with it once Sadie had been sick. After the second time, Tom slowed the truck so I could safely toss it out the window. It had been a good stocking cap, woven tightly with thick yarn.

Tom smelled of hay, and he did not wash the back of his neck. There was a plastic air freshener in the shape of a jumping dolphin hanging from the rearview mirror. He said he'd bought it because it reminded him of Sadie—so graceful, the joy. "You're a sweetheart, Tom," Sadie said. "You woo so well." Her voice cracked from her yells and shrieks, her cowgirl antics on the dance floor.

They'd met at a K-Mart while Sadie sifted through the packages of leftover Halloween candy. This was during a weekend I'd stood her up and she'd gone home to visit her mother. He had been an aisle over, contemplating motor oil. She'd been a comfort.

I had not known they were dating. These months I'd thought only that I'd finally taught Sadie her role in my new life, which was not much of one. My inclination is to erase that last sentence, or to soften it. But I reveal only more selfishness when I try: I understood my desire to be separated from her as little as I understood the cause for our friendship. I thought only of how much more time I had once she was gone, how much I had developed beyond her, the wide-stretching solitude I felt without her.

*

When Tom pulled into the driveway, Sadie was asleep on my shoulder. The radio played a love song from some group that had been popular seven years before. Tom killed the engine. The lights were on across the first floor of the house. Sadie stretched and said, "You know how I love that band."

"I thought you'd been joking," I said.

"I cried when I went to their concert," she told Tom. "I was sure I would marry one of them."

Through window sheers, I could see Aunt Kay's silhouette. I'd thought she'd be asleep. She walked to pick her drink from the coffee table. She wore pants with wide, flowing legs and kept her hips jutted forward. That was her way in pants. These were a gift brought from one of Mike's trips. There was a belt that tied in a big bow to the side, and one night I'd watched Mike twirl an end with his finger while we sat around, waiting for Ryan to finish discussing his dissertation.

"Wait," I told them. Aunt Kay had parted the sheers wide. She leaned with her hands on either side of the bay window frame. Her powdered face was brightly lit, impassive. The strange truck with its fading racing stripes did not trouble her. I realized as I stepped down that she would not be alone. If I opened her garage, I would find Mike's Lincoln. There would be music playing in the house, strings, and Mike would have turned on the nightly newscast, only to leave the room and finish some work on the Macintosh he kept in her study. So her boredom with Mike had become a deep and abiding river—so what? I could almost hear the flat force of her voice by the look on her face as she watched through the window. That is how I've come to understand this night. She turned to let me in the front door.

"Change your clothes," she said. "Get comfortable."

She thought, perhaps, that I had brought them here with a purpose. That she had cultivated my intuition to dovetail with her own.

She hadn't. But here I was, listening to her. I could have turned, told Tom and Sadie to leave, find some other place, some hotel, to spend the night. Instead, I walked in without giving them so much as a wave and undressed in the bathroom, taking the time to brush out my hair and tie it back. I put on cold cream for the first time, and one of Aunt Kay's silken kimonos. There was nothing else in the room to wear. I tied it around twice with red cord.

She had invited the two in. Tom sat on the edge of a couch cushion. He rested his elbows on his knees as if he were afraid to fall in. Sadie sat beside him with her legs up and tucked to the side. She'd wrapped a blanket around herself, across her shoulders and up to her chin. Aunt Kay placed etched glass tumblers on the table in front of them and poured the zinfandel she'd been saving.

"Apologies if it's not what you're used to," she said, and pulled out a footstool to sit on. It looked as if she were about to shine Tom's lugged boots. "It's all I have, and in my situation, I hardly entertain much."

"No need to entertain me," Tom said. He laughed. When he saw me, he nodded and poured a drink for me. He could not know what that pour had cost. The glass was small in his hand, and I could see the red hair of his knuckles against the crystal. "I suppose I'm more of a beer man these days."

"To Sadie," Aunt Kay said, and raised her glass. I sat on the far end of the room in a high-backed chair and got comfortable. We all drank.

"He's so sweet," Sadie said. She was continuing a conversation. Her voice broke. "He's been a wreck all week just about meeting Lottie." She laughed until she coughed. "He's really good for me," she said.

I heard Mike open the study door. There was a sigh. He walked down the hall and turned the corner into the room.

"Home already?" he said to me, and tossed his boxy phone onto the couch, where it landed on the cushion behind Tom's back, and Tom managed not to notice, admiring so deeply Sadie's bitten down nail beds as she sang his praises to my aunt. Mike waited for my accounting. The man could wait. There was no impatience in him. He settled that pale-eyed gaze on me. After years of knowing him, I believe this is his true business secret: regarding others as though he were some Greek icon awaiting confession, measuring penance, that air of gold about him.

I shrugged. "It was an early night."

He took a deep breath. Something had changed. "Isn't that your aunt's bathrobe?" he asked.

"And doesn't it *suit* her?" my aunt said from her footstool. Her legs were spread wide, like she was some peasant peeling potatoes. She waved her arm back at me without turning to look. Mike did not see Sadie and Tom—I mean, he did not understand what my aunt was staging—until she spoke again to Sadie.

"You should know," Aunt Kay said, and clinked her tumbler to Sadie's, "that it's all downhill from here." This was the kind of thing she said when she felt vindictive—drank much, *told it like it was,* spoke frankly to the notably attractive or outcast or powerful to show Mike he was not the boss. "You'll never love each other more than you do now."

"That's exactly how it feels," Sadie said. She leaned her head on Tom's ham-hock shoulder. "I can't imagine it gets any better."

It was the gentle familiarity that made her slow to react, and not the booze. The comforts of conversation, a good wine, the woven blanket, and the way her father strode about another place he owned. She was excited to see him. "Dad," she said. When she leaned across Tom to take her father's hand—a drunken gesture, I'd not seen it before—the blanket fell across her lap and her shoulders were bare. Her top had ridden up and there was a neat bulge of belly with a silver ring through the navel. The dark lipstick had worn off from the inside of her lips, and her chapped patches were stained red from the zinfandel.

Before Mike could react, my aunt said, "Michael, Sadie would like us all to go on a double—no—a triple date soon." She bent and gave one of Tom's bootlaces a yank. A thoughtless flirtation, a casual meanness: what else could she reach with her mischievous hands? "Yes," she said, "we think you'll be very comfortable here, Tom. A triple date, isn't that right, Sadie?"

Sadie nodded—less a nod than a churning—and my aunt laughed as though Sadie had told a joke. Tom had fallen back into the couch and kept his hands resting on his knees. He was as good as wallpaper.

"You'll have to check with Ryan about dates," she tossed back toward me. "And, Michael, you'll have to make sure your wife knows not to schedule anything, not that she would." She did not look at Mike.

"You can join our little club, Sadie," my aunt continued. She was digging a hole and could not be stopped until she'd thrown the dirt all around. Until the list of betrayals was made clear. As I watched her, I saw my future self, angry at having made so many of the wrong choices in life, lashing out for being powerless. It was only a deepening understanding. I'd known what I would become for some time. Mike sat on the edge of the footstool and pressed in until my aunt had to give up her throne and sat, instead, on his lap. He put his arm around her and, without a pause, held his hand out to Tom. "What's your field, Tom?" he asked. My aunt leaned her head on Mike's shoulder. Sadie looked to me, but as usual, I had nothing for her.

*

It was eight years before Sadie and Tom married, long enough for Tom to finish medical school and land a residency. Those had been Mike's terms. He could not have his daughter marrying a farmer. I lived then with Ryan in Madison. My aunt had found classes for us to teach at the university, and in summers I tended bar. Enough to live a life of noble debt, but Mike kept us a rung or two higher. "For his sake as much as yours," my aunt said. I was not sure whether she meant us to feel better about the money, or to bring us to her level.

We still spent evenings at Aunt Kay and Mike's house, ate steak bloody. Aunt Kay and I began walking together most evenings along the lake. Of all the clichés we felt we had avoided through intellect, we could not defy sagging, dimpling. Nature will run its course. On the first of these outings, I mentioned that my father and mother had walked along the lake when they were students at the university. My father had said it was a cheap date.

"Your father," she said, "is the kind of person who had talent and worked hard. He followed the rules and things turned out wonderfully for him." She said it as though there were something wrong with this.

"That is why he's in a dream world. He's living a fantasy."

As Sadie's wedding date approached, I spent more time with my aunt and took to sleeping over some nights, though Ryan and I lived only a few miles away. Mike was gone, running through the venue with his wife, reviewing the order for salmon. I liked the way we were without the men around. A little crass, flighty. I bathed there and used salts and droppers full of oil, imagining I had earned it, imagining that either of us deserved such things. Sadie and I had fallen further out of touch. We were acquaintances. I knew what Ryan told me, as he had become Tom's best man—both for the wedding and in life. Mike had arranged for them to have drinks years ago, and the introduction had stuck. "It's just that easy, Lot," Ryan took to saying. "You say you'll do something, and then you do it." He said it as though I were some flake. He had lost all patience for me.

*

The day after Sadie's wedding, I met my aunt at her house for breakfast. I'd attended the wedding as Ryan's wife and left the reception early.

I saw Sadie in the lobby before I left. She was with a friend from her new life. They were whispering. Sadie smiled, and her friend laughed. A simple white cloth covered all of the tables and her mother had embroidered the ends with white crosses. Sadie called to me, tipsy, and stumbled on her skirt. She embraced me. The flowers of her bouquet brushed my back. "Oh," she said, and trembled.

"I thought of everything but Sadie," I told my aunt.

I'd been seeing an older man, an Irish poet, for some time. We often went to the bar. There, he would shout at me, "Don't lead a middle-class life!" That was his reaction to my life: urgency, fear. I did not think much about Sadie for those eight years before her wedding, or miss her, or attempt forgiveness. When I saw her in that lobby, a wild grief or something like it shot through me. I could not be near her.

"It's hard to know what they see in us," my aunt said. "I don't know why they keep us around."

These are the kinds of questions I ask my students: What does A see in X or Y character? Who is responsible for Q? If the character wasn't focused on Z, what was she focused on? I do not expect answers, but I do expect them to try.

Hunting the Rut

The Bull

Wild steers run over the father's land. They tear through fences and drive the cows mad with their snorting and prancing. There is a bull, too. A red-haired giant with a yellowed face and belly. The bull charges, head down, horns pointed, at the father. This bull, the father thinks, is too much. He opens the truck cab, pulls out his Remington, and plugs four in the beast.

Before his hooves stop their slow thundering across the snow, the bull owns how he'll be slit up the middle, rectum to brisket, and spilled across the ground. His hooves cast aside, left to clack against themselves. On Sundays, he'll be roast with potatoes, rosemary, and soft peeled carrots. There is a final, envious, sexual twang for the couples that will tumble onto his hide, which will be ripped away from the muscle for a rug or a blanket. The father sees the bull give it all up before he falls at the father's feet, the force and the weight of him snapping the neck, not that this is necessary. The father's aim is exquisite.

The gunshot drives the steers over the hill, back to the neighbor's pasture from where they broke free. Blackbirds settle again into the tree branches. Cows attend to the sun-browned cornstalks that pop in rows through the snow. They munch, and the afternoon is quiet and growing late. The father turns to his truck for his knife. There is his daughter sitting in the cab, her back pressed up against the driver's side door, braced like she is still waiting for the bull to hit. But she is staring at him and not the bull.

The father shoulders his rifle and watches the last of the steers run off. He drove Hazel here to show how he had graded the land since she'd been gone—flattened the hills, filled the swamps. He wants her to stare, and so he acts as if this killing were effortless. To be in awe of him, that's why he drove her out here, to note that he can move mountains. But this. She hasn't stared at him like this for ages. Hush. Out here, it is so still a baby could sleep. He holds the silence. In it, she is rooted to him. She is not to be disturbed.

A calf bellers for his mother. Hazel relaxes behind the wheel. "That was a close one," she says.

"Hand me my knife."

She tosses him the knife in its pouch and climbs out of the truck. She slams the door. It doesn't catch. The lock's been rusted and broken since she was a teenager. She tries again, really puts some weight into it, and loses her footing. She falls into the snow. The door creaks shut. Snow melts through her long johns. She stands and brushes the clumps off. They were just sitting around the house when her father said he'd take them out back. She threw on some four-buckle boots and a letterman's jacket from the back of the closet. The jacket collar smells like the cologne a boyfriend used to wear. Which one? Mustang? Biceps? Or Jack. Could this really be Jack's? She takes another sniff. Everything from the closet smells like hay and cigarettes. She put on just enough clothing for a truck ride. She wasn't planning to roll in the snow. Jack wanted her to put on more—a stocking cap, earmuffs, something. He wouldn't come with them because he counted the beers her father had at lunch. He needs to learn not to count. She gave him a look. "It's just out back," she said, like it was a hint. Her father didn't give him any look. Jack was there to earn her father's blessing. Instead he is on the back porch, chain-smoking with her mother. Not that Ginny doesn't need a little sympathy. She does. Last time, the steers trampled the blackberry bushes. *No berries!* her mother is probably saying right now, pointing to the fleshy, torn-up brambles. They'll never have any berries.

Hazel looks in the truck bed for a clean bucket. There isn't one. She dumps a half-inch of silage and pellets from one to another and climbs down the wheel well. The bull is opened and rolled. Legs spread like a starfish. Steam rises from the stew of it. Her father kneels over him. When he's finished, he makes a ball of snow and runs his knife across it until the knife's clean and the snow's all melted. Hazel leans and looks over what's been dumped, like a woman looking for a ripe grapefruit at the grocery. There it is. She nudges the heart with her boot.

"Hey, throw that in here," she says.

"What for?"

"I'm gonna cook it."

He takes his knife back out and cuts the heart from the fat. That's his daughter. *His,* Jack. The heart's six pounds, maybe seven. It's still thrumming—has he ever felt this before?—so he holds it, waiting it out, until he lets it plop into the bucket. The bucket's inside is dusty with farm, and bits of straw are already stuck to the heart. He takes it from Hazel and stands away from the bull. He puts in fistfuls of clean snow, packing the heart like a present wrapped in tissue, and gives it back to her. "Thanks," she says. She walks back to the cab, the bucket held in front of her with two hands as if it's already dinner on a platter—like she is four again and they are playing dinner in the living room with plastic forks and fish that break in two at Velcro seams. Her long johns are wet through.

They chain the bull up to the truck by its hocks and drag it home slow, on its back, staining the snow all the way. Deer season starts tomorrow.

The Blood

The father pulls the truck up to the garage and swings it around the cement pad, so that the bull is right up on there. The truck's headlights quit on him last year—easy to fix, just a fuse—but he's found he doesn't need them. He feels his way across the farm. There is not a thing in its place without his putting it in that place. Including this bull. Other things crowd his mind: chores, putting up the deer stands, oiling the guns, taking down the scarecrow, teaching Jack to shoot before five a.m., calls to make: the neighbor, the insurance company, the butcher: cuts of meat, half-pound patties, jerky, sausages, sticks, seasonings. But first, the display.

Hazel jumps from the truck and makes for the garage. She flips on the floodlights and opens the house door. "The bull! He shot the bull!" she hollers. Once she hears Barcalounger footrests clunking down, she slams the door and runs back out to the truck. The lights shine down on the bull, his splayed forelegs, the tongue sticking from his mouth, the shot-out eye. Debauched. He's tough to stomach now that he's bled. Her father's cap is in his hands. His hair is messed. The wind picks up and now they can hear, from the field, the scarecrow with its back of windmill blades, punched and strung to clatter. Its body and arms are a shovel and a hoe. It's dressed in the father's clothes. Where was the wind two hours ago? The bull would be back over the ridge. Now he's public down to the backbone. Jack and her mother yak all the way through the garage. Hazel takes one of the bull's hind legs and tries to thrust him shut, but it's too late. He's rigid.

The first thing Jack sees is Hazel. "Hey, that's my old jacket," he says. Maroon with a white-striped collar. Why didn't he notice it when she was leaving? Because she had no hat. He looks up from the jacket. Still no hat. Her ears are red. He could give them a flick and they'd probably fall off. With his fingertips he outlines the gold P embroidered on the breast of the jacket, which, he realizes, is also Hazel's breast. He pulls his hand back. This is the jacket that won her over—the letter pins, the cologne. "Let's switch," he says. "I want to see if this puppy still fits." He whips off his coat, then unbuttons his jacket from Hazel and slides it down from her back. She is no help sometimes. A tank top! That is all she has on underneath. She holds her arms across herself and stomps one of her rubber boots. A sweater. She could have at least worn a sweater out. He wraps his coat around her and zips it up to her chin, pulling the collar up to her sweet, pink cheeks. Adorable. One arm slides into the letterman's jacket, then the other. It snaps up, no problem. "Perfect," he says. "Perfect fit." He looks around at all of them, waiting.

"Get that bull off the pad," Ginny tells the father. She lights a cigarette. "You'll stain the cement." But the father is sure that his daughter has just been fondled in front of him. The boy stands with his arms outspread, not noticing the blood that's smeared across his tan pants and the backs of his hands from the jacket. This is the boy his daughter has brought home. The father should deal him one. He will. If not now, later. He has been lurking around since high school, but now he is staying overnight. On their couch. That is where both his son- and daughter-in-law used to stay. It is part of the progression. He's worming his way in. "It still fits," the boy says. His daughter in her wet long johns. How has the father failed her? He must have done something wrong. "Do you hear me?" Ginny asks. "Get it off the cement." She smokes cigarettes like they're joints and not cigarettes. He can't understand this—does his wife have a secret and wild past? Had he interrupted it? He wanted to ask her this on their first date all those years ago, but he couldn't get the phrasing right. He didn't want to sound too curious. He needed to stay on top of the conversation. Who knows what she would have said. He could've been thrown.

He killed this bull. Has no one seen?

"Will you look at that," Jack says. He parades himself over to it, thumbs hooked in his jacket pockets. "What happened here?"

"The cement won't stain," the father says. He climbs into the cab and starts the engine. The truck rolls down the driveway, the bull stretched behind it. The heart. Hazel jogs after the truck, grabs onto the door handle, and hoists herself up. She knocks on the window and then opens the door. "Supper," she says. She takes the bucket by the handle. The snow's pink and icy.

Ginny smokes and watches the truck inch its way toward the barn. Hazel takes the heart inside. Jack stays put. The father is burying the bull. The butcher shop is closed till morning, but then it will be full. Ginny tried to tell him, but he drove away. She is only trying to help. Momma tried—write that on her tombstone. The shop will be too full with deer. It is every year. He shovels deep into the far snowbank. The truck is still running, pumping out exhaust. She swears to Jack that she can smell the diesel burning from here. She coughs to prove the point. She gathers it up in the back of her throat and spits it on the cement. What does Jack care if she spits? He's been around a decade, maybe longer. The spit doesn't freeze. It's packing snow—the father should know that. It's too warm for this business. He pulls the bull into the trench with the truck. He scoops snow overtop until all that's left is a hoof hanging out. The meat will rot. Please, Lord, don't let the meat rot. But he'd better plan on two deer at least. A buck and a doe. He has tags for both. Jack has one tag—three deer? Less likely. The scarecrow clanks, clanks—he'd better take down the scarecrow, too. The freezer's getting empty. Everything at the grocery is dripping with hormones. She saw a *Dateline* special on it. The men are growing breasts. She looks over at Jack and takes a puff on her Marlboro. He's a good boy with a real job—a geologist, a university job. Cushy, with an office. But no gun skills: two deer.

The Heart

Hazel dumps the heart in the sink and gets the hot water running over it. The bucket goes out to the garage. With a paring knife, she slices out the arteries, cuts away some fat. She slits it down the side and rinses and keeps rinsing. The water is superb. She lets the heart drain on a plate, leaves the plate in the sink. Jack will not like the look of it.

She watches him take his jacket off. His t-shirt sleeve has bunched up to his armpit because the jacket no longer fits him. He's grown huge from the gym. She sometimes likes to knock on his biceps, his pecs, as if on a door. *Who's there?* she says. Ginny stands between them, kicking off her shoes. Jack fumbles to roll the shirtsleeve down. *Hazel* is tattooed under his arm. He got it done at a place like a doctor's office. It is small and cursive and blends in with his underarm hair. He's become fussy about covering it. He doesn't want to make the wrong impression.

When Jack sees that Hazel's feet are blue-white and crossed, one arch on top of the other, he wants to take them in his hands and rub them warm. She holds a wooden spoon, rests it against her shoulder. Barefoot in the kitchen. And still wet-through. She should shower, bundle up. Jack follows Ginny as she makes her way into the living room. They are discussing the blackberry bushes. He is here to get their blessing. He is patient. The bushes are trampled, the fences need mending, the headlights, fixing—the meat will rot. He says, "Yes. It's a shame. A dirty rotten shame." The father is more difficult. That is why they are hunting tomorrow: to bond. Sometimes, he feels like he could just ball up his fist and—

Hazel grabs the back of his t-shirt. She pulls his head down close, her cold hands through his hair, and whispers in his ear. "Wash your hands." She has read his mind, is scolding him, playing homemaker—domestic bliss. "There's blood on them," she says. He looks down. There it is, dark on his hands, the front of his pants. What has he done? "From the jacket." Why didn't he notice?

He walks off to the shower, still looking at his hands. Hazel slaps him from behind with the spoon.

The footrest comes up in the living room. "Where's Jack?"

The crockpot is here; the mixing bowls, there. Hazel uncorks a bottle of red—she and Jack brought three as a gift. She thought it would help. She pours herself a coffee-cupful to fight the chill. In a bowl, she puts breadcrumbs. She has had heart only once before. A science teacher made it for them in grade school. It was part of a lesson. Hazel knocks the recipe together: minces a big bulb of garlic, slices an onion. Throws them in with the crumbs. Pepper, salt, bay leaves she found in a baggie in the back of the pantry. The teacher said it was the most tender meat they would ever taste. Hazel ate a slice off a toothpick. Students often cried in the classroom. That day was no different. The teacher did not withhold judgment. In a saucepan, Hazel melts a stick of butter, then pours it into the bowl and mixes. The heart was delicious. She felt brutal eating it, and the feeling made her nervous. She took only the one bite and began to hiccup so loudly that the teacher stopped class and said it would not go on until Hazel made herself quit. Hazel fills her coffee cup again. The teacher was a favorite of hers, and she the teacher's. She shakes the last of the water from the heart. Her father cut it out effortlessly, as if it, and the shooting, and the gutting were something often done. She stuffs in the buttery mix. She wraps the heart closed with lengths of string. What's left of the wine gets poured in the crockpot, along with a can of beef broth. She drops it in. High heat, two hours. Or three on medium. She doesn't know. High to start. She needs a hot shower.

The Wine

For three minutes, Jack and Hazel can't get enough of each other in the bathroom. The front door slams—the father is in. They part as if nothing were happening. Jack picks his dirty clothes from the floor. Hazel wipes steam from the mirror.

The father does not mean to slam the door, but he always does. Outside, inside—it's hard to adjust the motions. He calls his neighbor. The phone rings and rings. The linoleum is cold, and there are holes in the father's socks. He leaves a message. The gist: your bull's dead. He calls the butcher. He uncorks a bottle of wine and has a coffee-cupful to put off the chill. He calls insurance. Jack comes in, his hair slick and parted. The insurance agent answers. Jack gets a glass and pours himself some wine. He asks Ginny if she'd like some. She wouldn't mind if she did. The call does not go well. The agent wants photos, accounts. Jack tells Ginny he cannot believe that the father didn't take pictures of the bull before the father buried him, before he gutted him. Usually, the boy talks so fast, the father can't understand a word he says. Tonight, he hears. Jack is right. The father would like to take a hammer to the side of the boy's knee. Ginny is over his shoulder. "The bushes, the fences," she calls. "Tell them about the scarecrow. Tell them you tried to stop them." The father lowers the mouthpiece to his shoulder and looks at his wife. "What's he say?" she asks. The father once spent an afternoon in the garage, writing her a poem.

"He asked if I couldn't keep my wife down," he says, and brings the phone back to his head.

Ginny nods to the place on the countertop where Jack should set her wine. Ginny threw the ring at the father before they even got married. She was leaving. She can't remember why, but she was. He was yukking it up, saying she'd never do it. No way was she leaving. Ginny threw the ring at him and took off in her little blue sports car. She bought it herself. Brand new, three thousand, give or take a hundred bucks. Whatever happened to that car? She motions for Jack to fill the glass—none of this fancy halfway stuff. The boy bought Hazel a cell phone last year. He worried too much about her, he said, when she was on the road.

When Hazel comes downstairs, they all look up. She smiles. But she has disappointed them. Her hair is stringy and wet. It drips, and a splotch grows across the back of another tank top. Plaid flannel pants rolled several times at the hip cover the tops of her feet. Does she not know how much they need her to be beautiful, to look fresh, and to be concerned for each of them? There is a zit on her chin, round as a dime, that she has just squeezed. She must not know.

Ginny raises her glass to Hazel and takes a drink. She remembers wearing feathered earrings and a gold shift dress that drove the father wild.

Jack looks the father down to his hole-bitten socks. He forgets that, two seconds ago, their thoughts ran parallel. A cruel man, he thinks, wife and now daughter flattened out with a look, a phrase. He's of half a mind to hook his ankle behind the father's and send him tumbling down to the—

"Get the gun," the father says.

The crockpot bubbles. It is too hot, Hazel thinks. It's not supposed to boil so much.

"Tomorrow," the father says. He pours another cupful of wine. He is both pleased and guilty. "Tomorrow, before we go out. I'll give you a crash course." He smiles and goes upstairs to shower.

Hazel lowers the heat on the pot. Steam rushes out, and Hazel feels the first lurch of hunger. She puts her hand on her hip bone. These pants are so large, she feels sickly thin in them. She could eat the whole potful herself. But the heart looks the same: raw, slightly ashen. Ginny sticks a meat fork through it and holds it up. Soggy breadcrumbs fall from the seams where Hazel stuffed it.

"Hazel, this won't be ready for hours."

"Not on high?"

"No." Ginny lets the heart plop back in its broth. Momma tried. "Set it to simmer," she says. "It won't be ready until tomorrow." She should have said something, but Hazel knows what she's doing—or so she says, all the time. Ginny pulls a jug of wine from the pantry and sets it on the countertop. "There's bread and eggs in the fridge."

Ginny goes out for a smoke.

Hazel stares at the jug and remembers trying to leave a party, not so long ago, when the man she'd been kissing hoisted her up on the countertop without stopping the kissing. They'd knocked over a jug and—

"How's the heart coming?" the father asks. He is still wiping his face dry with a hand towel, spreading his movements liberally throughout the rooms so that Jack and his belt buckle know whose house this is.

"It won't be ready until tomorrow," she says. "I'll have to pack it in your lunches." She looks at him the same way she did in the field, and so he doesn't say anything. Quiet, quietly, she's held to his attention. He brings the towel down to his side, and feels stupid for bringing it. Poor Jack. He doesn't have a chance. Is he seeing this? The father looks over. He is. The boy sees it.

"What about those guns?" Jack says.

"Yep," the father says. "We need to oil the guns." Hazel puts the lid on the crockpot. The juices start back to simmering.

The Night

Ginny sleeps like a rock. At midnight, Jack sneaks up into Hazel's room and then wonders why. She is passed out cold with a strange smile on her face. The father stirs and stirs. They forgot to put up the tree stands. The neighbor didn't call back.

At two, Hazel wakes up, ravenous. She sneaks from under Jack's arm and tiptoes downstairs. The heart is still bubbling. She will have just a bite, from the bottom. No one will know. She flips the heart with the meat fork, takes a knife and shaves a thin slice. She holds it on the fork, lets it cool, and eats. The meat is everything she remembered. She slices another and another. She cuts through to the breadcrumbs and takes a forkful. Then she turns the heart back over in the broth and replaces the lid. She stares outside the kitchen window until she goes back to bed.

At three, Jack is wide-awake. Not long ago, Hazel came back to bed forceful and energized. Now, she sleeps. He'll be outside with the father in no time at all. He rises from bed and eases himself down the stairs. An empty jug and three bottles of wine line the countertop. They used most of it cooking, Hazel said. A fork and a knife rest by the crockpot in a little puddle of juice. He's always lived in this town, but his family isn't the type to go hunting. He lifts the pot lid. He takes the knife and cuts quarter-sized chunks. They bubble at the top of the broth. He forks them in, one by one. He eats like he'll never get enough. When he's done, he flips the heart over to hide the crumbs spilling out, and goes back up to Hazel's bed.

The father gives up on sleep at four, a half hour before either his or Jack's alarm is set to go off. When he goes downstairs, the couch is empty. In the crockpot, breadcrumbs bubble at the top. The father gets a plate. He thinks of the empty couch while he sticks the meat fork through the heart, lets the broth drip from it, and begins to slice it by the quarter inch. He turns the pot off. Starts the percolator. He makes four sandwiches, each with a thick layer of stuffing and strips of meat. The bread is soaked through before he gets them in their baggies. He covers the rest of the heart with foil and puts it in the fridge. He pours the coffee in two short thermoses. At four-thirty, he stands outside Hazel's room in his blaze orange. The door opens.

"Let's go," the father says.

The Hunt

The men walk into the back forty. There is no wind and a fog has settled in overnight.

The snow is glazed and hard on top from melting. They fall through it with each step. Jack will not say anything about it, but the bull will rot. The father has a pace with which he can't keep up. Too fast of a pace for carrying a gun under the arm, which he is. There must be a manual that suggests a different way to carry it. The father should be on his way to the butcher's right now, like Ginny said. Yes, that's a better place for the father. Jack trips a little each time he raises his foot. He is sweating under the heavy orange jacket he has borrowed, but he doesn't dare unzip it. The birds have started to sing.

As the father walks, the rifle slips down. His vest is waterproof and slick. When the rifle slips, he pulls it back and repositions it. As he does this, he taps Jack in the hip with the butt of his gun. Jack pauses, then resumes pace. The father has the sandwiches stuffed two in each pocket. He's been looking forward to eating one all night. As soon as he is up in a tree, away from the boy, he will eat one, and save the second for after his first kill. The kitchen was filled with the heavy simmered smell, the rasping of the percolator. A beautiful morning. Jack's rifle is in a case, hanging from a strap slung across his shoulders. He carries a thermos in each hand so they don't clank, like the father told him. The boy is a good listener. They walk. It is so satisfying, walking in the morning air. The father takes his gun with both hands and jams it back into Jack's hip. The father keeps on. Jack stops for only a minute before he's beside the father again, limping. "The couch is lumpy. Ginny's been telling me that for years," the father says. The scarecrow is ahead of them. Its shovel head is covered with an orange stocking cap. An old flannel shirt hangs from the hoe stretched across. The windmill blades hang still like the ridges on a dragon's spine. They stop in front of it.

"The valley's a good spot," the father says. "Shoot to kill, otherwise you'll have to track through the brush to find it." Jack nods and stares at the scarecrow. It seems the only correct thing to do. Last night, the father set up pop cans along the porch railing and had Jack shoot them off from ten feet away, Jack's back up against the house. The father said he was a great shot. He was five for ten. Jack was proud of it until he woke up. When he saw the father, he felt he should rush back into the bedroom, shake Hazel awake, and tell her something. It was urgent. But he didn't know what it was. Instead, he went. "Fire two shots up in the air," the father says, "if you need help, if you're going inside, if you need to tell me something." On foggy mornings in late November, if there was still no snow, Jack and his father would sometimes golf using orange golf balls. His mother always worried about them. It really is the only color you can see out here. He looks from the scarecrow's stocking cap to the father's baseball cap. Both orange. Jack pulls the hood of his jacket up, over his head, and ties the strings tight. The father points to a tree behind Jack. "That's a good place to set up in," he says. Jack turns and looks up. The hood is muffling what the father is saying.

The father hooks his boot around Jack's ankle. He pushes Jack. The boy falls with his face in the snow.

This is what he's been expecting, of course. Permission. Jack's lip bleeds just a bit where it was chapped and cracked. He licks his lips and turns all the way up to a crouch before he wraps his arms around the father's thighs and throws him to the ground. This is his moment. He takes the father by the collar and shakes him once. *I will not let you go until you bless me,* Jack thinks. *It is what I came for and I will not let you go.* He shakes him a second time. The father takes his fist and punches Jack in his already sore hip. Jack drops. Recovers. They look each other in the eye. They both know Jack's limits. Then Jack turns and walks away. His socket feels thrown. He feels he'll never walk straight again, and yet he is. He defies the father to shoot. Go ahead. He walks until he gets to the tree and then he climbs it. The bark is thick and the branches hang low. The thermoses are back by the father. He can keep them. Let him clank.

Through the fog, Jack watches the father's outline walk through the field. Slow, steady progress, as if he came out here alone. Behind him, Jack hears something breaking through the woods. He turns. Two, three, many more shadows rush out across the white field. The steers, sans bull. They're charging through the valley, their hooves silent in the snow. Jack turns back to the father, and the father walks on. The father does not see what he has coming. Jack unzips the rifle from its case. His hands are shaking. Jack levels the rifle on his shoulder and sets his sight on the scarecrow's orange stocking cap. Then drops the sight—just a tad, down to the back—and fires. Once, twice, and again.

The windmill blades clang and clang. The whole valley is filled with their clanging. The cattle stop their stampeding. They scatter and run, back from where they came. The father has not moved. When the last of the cattle has gone over the hill, the father raises his Remington and fires twice into the clear air. The sign. That is enough. Jack leans back into the V of the tree trunk, to rest his head on the snowy bark, though it is only daybreak.

Love Me, and the World Is Mine

Theresa meets him at the tattoo parlor where she works as a receptionist. He gets a raven inked over his left shoulder blade. "A nightingale," Theresa says, when he turns his back toward her and makes the still-glistening thing swell by flexing. He turns and spits chew into the garbage basket beside her desk. His cheek bulges as his tongue rubs his jawbone clean. Theresa is sixteen. He waits in the parlor, flipping through magazines, until the parlor closes. Her boss gives him dirty looks. When they leave together, he slides a magazine into her bag. He puts his finger over his lips in a *shhh,* and then tickles her rib with that same finger. She laughs. The guy takes her to some place with strobing lights and the loudest music she has ever heard. He kisses her. He is rough with her.

In her bed that night, she tries to sleep. She can't tell if the roaring she hears is her heart, or if it's her ears, still echoing the bar. Every time she closes her eyes, her head feels like it's bouncing against the pillow. She feels a sharp pain in her right ear and when she brings her hand up to it, it is wet and sticky. Blood is clotted into her pillow's weave.

She walks up and down the hallway, her hair loose and smelling of smoke. There is no moon and it is dark except for a flickering nightlight hanging out of its socket. Her hand cups her ear. Her head cocked like a child's. She should wake Tillie, but she also shouldn't. Tillie would know what to do, but Tillie is also impossibly old: 198 by Tillie's calculations, and 79 by everyone else's. Because Tillie will die in two years, Theresa, as well as this story, humor her. Tillie's desires are simple, and her story is not one of unrealistic beauty, but one of unrealistic timeline. Tillie is an artist. She works with stained glass. Her delirium can be attributed to heartbreak, age, or the lead ribbons she works with daily. We must be kind to our artists. Many of them are poisoned by something or other.

Tillie's death will happen tragically, in public, while Theresa watches. Tillie has been preparing Theresa for her death from a young age. When Theresa misbehaved as a child, Tillie rarely yelled or hit her. She would play dead. When Tillie woke up, she would say, "You were being so bad, you nearly killed me. Then what would you do?" But while Tillie lay there on the living room floor, doll hairbrushes and high heels scattered around her, Theresa filled with fear. Once, Tillie let her head slam alongside her plate at the supper table. Hair, loose from her bun, fell in her creamed potatoes. Theresa shook her grandmother until the woman's arm fell limp from the table and hung by her side. Tillie didn't flinch through the screaming, and didn't come to until Theresa pulled a chair over to the phone, so she could reach it and call the fire squad. It was the worst punishment either could imagine, and it didn't have to be used very often. Each was the only person the other had left. Neither could make sense of anything without the other. The sense they did make was often off, informed by a logic they had created themselves from quiet nights flipping through magazines and long walks outdoors. Logic that fell along the line of: when I cross this cornstalk's shadow it will be noon. Most of the time, Theresa sat cow-eyed by her grandmother's side, eating ice cream with peanut butter and watching soap operas.

Theresa decides to knock, just so softly. Tillie might be waking up soon anyway. It is nearly three and she is an early riser, a frequent napper. Theresa's hand leaves smears on the wood. She wipes them with the bottom of her nightdress. *Tillie,* she whispers. Then, louder, *Tillie!*

And again, Tillie is pulled back into this old body. She is continually surprised to find herself alive. Surprised, also, to be shriveled. Before she wakes, she is always a girl in a skirt, grass-stained at the knees, peering into the dirt. It is 1818 and she holds her hands behind her back. What has just made her trip? She picks a stick from a patch of muddied leaves and pokes at the culprit: long and lying in the ground like an overgrown root, shining like a tin can or a yellow-bellied snake. She places the stick underneath and levers it up, out of the ground. And then a man appears. Before she can look at what she has dug up, he has taken it. Who is it? She isn't sure. She thinks it is a lover, but *Guess again, Tillie.* That is what the postcard says, the postcard she keeps on her desk, postmarked 1905. *Who's there?*

"It's me. Theresa."

*

St. John's Mine. The local mine where Tillie gathers lead for her stained glass. There, Tillie twines her history in and out. There, she becomes part of the land. The land is called the driftless zone. It, like Tillie, stays and gathers. Studies say the glaciers were averted. The ice collected the wealth of silt, lead, clay, gravel, boulders from the north, and, like an offering, buried it gently and deeply into the earth. The hills are rolling and vast with it. And then the icy sheets split, or melted in a rush down the Mississippi. Lead laces the bluffs. The ore is supple, weaving in and through, bulging like the veins of an old woman's hand—milky gray and waiting for the extraction.

Settlers could take a knife or a deer antler, anything, and pry the lead from the land. Out she came. This is how it was at first, that easy. Like a girl plucking arrowheads from the soft, tilled earth, following her father's plow in spring.

Feel lead's weight in your hand, the pull of your shoulder as you add to your pail. The ache in your back. Its richness. Feel the lead soak through the skin, enter your blood.

The 1820s—The Lead Rush and the Sale.

*

The girl's eardrum is ruptured. Tillie wraps her robe under her old breasts. Each year, this becomes more like bundling a sack of grain. Tillie has Theresa sit on the toilet seat—time has stolen Tillie's height—and she swabs the whorls of the ear and the side of the neck with cotton. There are bruises growing along the forearms that neither mentions. When the girl's skin is clean, Tillie tells her to change her nightdress.

Tillie puts the teakettle on, an hour earlier than usual. Each morning she drinks her first cup at 4:30. While drinking, she sits at the butcher's table and flips through *Snake Hollow: A Local History*, a book for which she was interviewed in the '80s, when the church ladies decided the town needed a proper history. She catches errors each time. The hot water is for the girl. It dawns on Tillie that Theresa will have to be married soon and to someone nearby. She cannot go wild and run off like her mother. It would break Tillie's heart, and Tillie cannot bear that happening again. When the kettle sings, she pours the water into a bowl with Epsom salts and twirls a towel in it. The water fogs Tillie's eyeglasses. She feels her way down the hall.

The pillowcase is clean. It must have been flipped. The girl is under the covers, lying on her side.

"This will be hot," Tillie says. Tillie hoists her stiff hip up onto the bed so that she sits behind Theresa. The bowl is between the two, and the water quivers near the brim. She twists Theresa's hair up, away from her face. She wrings out the towel over the bowl, then places it on her ear. The rest winds down her shoulder, which is fine. The girl is covered in goosebumps.

Tillie cups salty water onto the girl's towel until the sheets are soaked and she's sure Theresa is asleep. Tillie was married when she was Theresa's age. In reality, she was married to a man who owned a bar. But her dreamy existence, the one we are granting her in this story, hinges on being married to St. John, in 1820. Willis St. John was a big, broad-hipped man. The day he showed up at their house, Tillie looked down at him from an upstairs window. She wore the same pattern of nightdress that Theresa now wears: thin lines of rosettes running up and down between blue pinstripes. Tillie never changed out of her nightclothes unless she went to town or someone came to visit. This bothered her father, who, in those days, smelled constantly of shaving soap and new leather boots and belts. He didn't use to mind her laxness, but the lead she'd found near the cave had made them something like society. She was not expecting St. John, so she hid in the bedroom and watched what she could. She listened, pressed to the floorboards—they cushioned everything, and so it was hard to hear their visitor. His voice was soft and lilting. Tillie wanted him to go on talking. He came to buy their land, her father told her once St. John left. He came to buy the land the cave was on, her father repeated, and he was looking for a wife.

Tillie pinned up her hair and took a bird bath. She swept the house out. She put cornbread in the oven. When she finished all she could think of to do, she nodded to herself: so it could be done, after all. It was an early spring and the animals were confused. Raccoon dug through their gardens, finding nothing. All night long, Tillie lay in bed, listening to the summer birds sing their morning songs and crickets rub their legs together.

*

Lumbermen from Kickapoo, teamsters from Missouri and Cornwall, the Germans raised camps from the valleys and named this place Snake Hollow. The Black Hawk War fought itself out all around them. The lead that lay about like plant roots was collected and grew beyond its pails, straight to the stock exchange. Better than the potato eyes set in water to feed a man's children through the winter.

Then they craved its core. They felt they had almost, already, found it. Bitten miners, out in pairs, canvassed with chisels and sledgehammers, picking deeper, pecking holes for ore that once covered the land like rotting apples pigs could feed on.

They struck matches. The earth lurched with dynamite, their convincing it, their wooing it. They needed it. Limestone curtains ripped open. All manner of wealth was revealed.

They hereby christened this cave St. John's (after Willis St. John, who would make several bad investments). The cave gave 200 tons of ore those years leading up to the 1850s, before they hit the water table—but there was gold in California. Prospects.

*

But first, Tillie knows, there was this: late afternoon, and Tillie took a long bath. The water was cold before she got out. She braided her hair and twisted it around her head in a crown, then dabbed rosewater behind her ears, between her breasts. The rosewater was a gift from her father, sent for from New York, and so was the dress she put on next, which was a red she had seen before only on actresses in the cinema advertisements that floated, sometimes, through town. When it was dark, she went downstairs. Her father was at the table, looking at the advertisements in *The News-Letter.* When he saw his daughter, he nodded, pleased, and lit a lantern for her.

The grass was dewy. She was not wearing shoes. She knew the fields and the flat-rock path through the trees. The night was blue, not black. The silhouettes of deer and rabbits made quick in front of her. At the cave, she found St. John asleep. Near his head lay his belt, a silver pocket watch, and a pistol. His boots were set beside his feet. Several canvas bags of tools and dynamite were scattered near the wet cave walls. He slept on his back in a pressed white shirt, a wool blanket pulled to his chest. Tillie blew the light out and entered the cave. She folded his blanket down to his feet and lay beside him without touching him. He breathed as quietly as he slept. They were married the next week.

*

For a full minute, Theresa feels beautiful. Like a girl woken in the snow after being left frozen for many years. The sun shines between the blinds, onto the salts that have dried into a lace along her eyelashes and frosted the ends of her twisted hair. The room is a-sparkle and hazy at once. The bedsheets hold her crisply until she rips her sleeves away.

In the bathroom, she takes a washcloth and tries to wash the salt away. When she is finished, her skin is flushed and raked from it. She talks into the mirror: "I can't hear. I can't hear myself," to see if it's true. And it is, in part. She leans to the side and hits her good ear with her open palm, in case it is just trapped water. Nothing comes out.

She goes to Tillie, who is in the den working on her correspondence, as she does every morning until noon. She gives the letters to Theresa to mail at the end of each day. Theresa throws them away. Everyone Tillie writes to is dead, and the addresses are never more than a name and a city. Like the postcard Tillie takes out every morning: *Mrs. Tillie, Snake Hollow, Wisconsin.* It was sent from Kinzie Street, Chicago, in 1915. On the front is an Asti painting, *Portia:* a softened portrait of a woman looking off to the west. Her skin is so pale it is hard to tell where the white of her dress and her chest meet. She wears a claret shawl and cap that brings out the blush of her cheek and parted lips. Her hair is wild. *LOVE ME, AND THE WORLD IS MINE* is typeset in a deep blue across her breast.

Theresa always feels this soft-lipped *Portia* on the postcard could reach out and touch her lover, grab his shirtfront and pull him in. He is that close, the man the woman loves. He might even be Asti, the painter. But he never enters the picture. He remains offstage, going about his business. The back of the card reads *Just a pleasant reminder of your favorite song. Guess again, Tillie.* And though Theresa is half-deaf this morning, she can almost hear the song, "Love Me and the World is Mine," playing on the gramophone. Tillie hears it always. It was a favorite in her family, and the song, like Tillie's name, has been passed down. But Tillie doesn't remember this family, not its tastes or her generations of namesakes. She thinks only of St. John, and only St. John could fashion a song so perfect for their love: *I care not for the stars that shine; I dare not hope to e'er be thine.* When Tillie puts down her pen and turns to Theresa, Theresa falls to tears.

*

In the first years, when it became dark and St. John had not yet come home, Tillie would start to think something had happened at the mine. All day long she would walk around her new little house and listen to the dynamite explode, and the clunking of man-barrels up and down against the cave walls, and a constant sound like woodpeckers. Hollering. Sundown, she would sit on their front step picking at her feet until she heard his song through the trees. *I wander on as in a dream, my goal a paradise must be. . . .* And then she felt jealous, always, of his happiness, until she saw him shake the silvery dust from his boots into a neat pile. The first night this happened, he pointed to it and said, "This is more than a full dollar's worth of lead." He bent over and blew it out like a candle. It caught in the dew, and the grass was aglow with it. He laughed and held her waist to his and spun her around, singing, "We're rich! We're rich, Tillie!" And Tillie murmured into his warm neck, "We are, we are."

For their tenth anniversary, St. John fashioned miniature wooden baskets and set peonies and lead bits the size of teeth in them. She set them on either side of the window, which was hung with lace sent for from Alsace. She saw him almost always at night, when she was already in bed. He became so pale. Tillie would watch him as he undressed. When he slid into bed and encircled her, she would act as if she'd been asleep and say, "Don't scare me like that." Then she would lift her arms. Her nightdress came off as easy as the skin off a snake.

St. John set up a saloon across from the tack shop on the main drag and had Laurie, a lamed miner, run the bar. They kept the beer in the cave where it was cool, and they hired a thick-thighed boy to pull the kegs with a wooden cart up to the saloon. Tillie went there once, before St. John came home for the night. From their house she could just hear the rowdy, out-of-tune piano. The rare shouts made the deer freeze in the woods. There was no hiding from the new noise. St. John didn't want to take her there.

She wore the dress her father had sent for when she was just a girl. She had never seen so many men together in the same place. She was still standing in the doorway when one, falling, grabbed her dress to catch himself. Her dress ripped in two places where the man had grasped: her bodice and the top of the skirt. "It was an old dress," Tillie kept saying as St. John walked her home, holding on to her arm.

Each week St. John had money coming in from Laurie and from the mine. When Tillie woke in the morning, she would find large prepared envelopes and packages left on the table for her to send to New York. She did. She visited her father and with him ate large plates of pancakes for the coming baby. The company was good, and she went for as long as he was alive.

She took up stained glass to fill the day, after St. John's shirts were ironed, holding the glass together with lead ribbons. She melted the thick ribbons from odd pieces of lead she gathered around the house. She built clumsy windows and panels, embedded glass into flat stones. She took down her window lace. All the glass was green or brown or clear—stuff broken from peroxide bottles, or emptied flasks she found in St. John's pockets. It was wonderful, breaking them all. Shaping the glass into a hummingbird, a wheat field, a pickax, an outline of a heart—an anatomy lesson for the other miners' wives who are left in '49, for the gold rush. And St. John with them, to California, to pay debts.

*

The population dropped from thousands to hundreds. Businesses closed. Boundaries, lost. Everything grew wide from lack of use: roads, fields, women. Birds sat and sat at the tops of bluffs and watched the river roll by. Chicago grew large, or so they heard. The post office was stacked with letters for people who took off for big places. One day, the postmaster lit an incredible fire in his yard and got rid of it. He told no one, but for months after the land was scattered with pieces of family photos and *Say, brother, I bought that plot* . . . and *Mother's asking* . . . and *The flowers came up early this year* . . . and *Can't wait* . . . *Wouldn't believe* . . . *Won't you come home yet? Mary bought a new dotted dress and is waiting for you.*

So that the territory didn't disappear, they made themselves useful. There was no lead left. They tried bulk grain, hops. They floated beer in kegs down the river to Dubuque, St. Louis, New Orleans. Invented plows. Filled train cars with corn, oats, coal. They birthed Harry Houdini. *See?* they said. They were needed. They planked timber. Aged whisky. Quarried limestone. Jellies. Furs. Leather. Smoked meats. The beautiful daughters were shipped to New York or California to be silent-film stars. The smart ones were sent places, too. There were, of course, losses.

*

Afternoon, and the guy from the tattoo parlor comes knocking at the door. Tillie stands over the stove, a spatula poised to flip three thick pancakes. Theresa sits at the table. Maple syrup smeared across her left cheek. She has been dipping saltines in syrup, unable to wait for the cakes. Tillie drops the spatula in the skillet. She mimes knocking and says, "There's someone at the door." Theresa tiptoes toward the window. There is the Ford Escort she got a ride home in last night, the Happy Joe's Pizza logo still visible under a coat of black paint. He is wearing a t-shirt with the sleeves cut off so low, his ribs show. Theresa can see the corner of a bandage over his shoulder blade, where his work from the night before is probably oozing right now. "It's him," Theresa says, and both the women make for Theresa's bedroom, where the blinds are drawn. They sit on the floor under the window. Tillie, still in her robe. Theresa, still in her nightdress.

"And just who is *he?*" Tillie says. Her smile is, she knows, sly. She wants to show Theresa this is how love works. She rubs the girl's arm, squeezes her cold, sticky hand. Theresa lets her head hit the wall. She lets it hit the wall again. Theresa is a late bloomer. Too shy. Maybe, Tillie thinks, she has neglected Theresa. Tillie is right to think this, and it extends beyond the girl's hair, which Tillie is thinking should be brushed out and put up for once, none of this limp, hanging business, falling over the eyes. Tillie's neglect will shadow all of Theresa's future relationships, which will be few, and the few will be unhealthy. No one can love Theresa in the way Tillie does. Here, the neediness is reciprocal. It has grown organically out of a shared situation like a language forms its letters. Elsewhere, it becomes baggage. Tillie lets her hand go and tucks Theresa's bangs behind her ear. Theresa stares ahead as if she doesn't notice. If this one works out, if it can be arranged, Tillie thinks, she will get to keep her. She will move into a house just a walk away. They will never be apart.

He pounds on the door again. Theresa can feel it through the wall this time. A stained-glass hummingbird, suspended, sucking nectar from a peony, falls from behind the blind. Cracks, Theresa is sure. It has been on her window for as long as Theresa can remember. Tillie made it. There are birds like it all over town. Theresa is fond of it. She would look out at the cornfields at night or in a storm and expect something strange to come out from between the rows: an animal or a ghost or a boogieman. When she started to scare herself, she would turn to the bird and hear a soft fluttering of wings.

Tillie grabs her arm and says, "He says he wants his stuff back." Then, "What does he mean?"

Theresa shakes her head. "I don't have anything." She can just hear his car door slam, and can picture his backing up, his throwing it into drive, the gravel spinning out. The pancakes are burnt.

*

In 1910, one of Tillie's imaginary daughters came home from the high school dance, moonstruck. She spun herself in small, dazy circles, as if the sailor who was her date stood there still, admiring the gauze of her dress billowing out against his starched uniform. She sang the song under her breath, *Suns may shine to light my way, dear,* kept time to it.

Tillie sat at the butcher's table, steaming her face over a mug of tea. She hummed herself along into a reverie. Then stopped short. "Where'd you learn that song?" she asked. Her daughter paused, her hand still raised overhead mid-turn, her back arched. "At the dance," she said. "They have a record player." Then she peeled back in to her unseen partner and swayed.

That November, Tillie took the emergency money from the flour sack under her mattress and went to Chicago with the neighboring farmer when he went to sell his bulk oats. She bought a gramophone and three records, including the song her daughter sang, "Love Me, and the World is Mine," but now, instead of St. John singing it sweetly through the woods, a stiff-collared man sang it in a deep vibrato with an orchestra. The store clerk insisted she couldn't buy just one record, so she bought two more, some things the clerk said were popular, and that didn't cost much. She sat with it all on her lap the whole way home, even though, the farmer showed her, there was plenty of room for it between Tillie and himself. Tillie's children quickly grew sick of her record singing them to sleep every night and would beg her to play those other records. There was a jitterbug and a waltz, and sometimes Tillie would have them dance with her, to show her the steps. But her joints were swollen, and she was a clumsy dancer. She watched.

Around this time, Tillie got the postcard in the mail, the one with the painting of *Portia* on the front. She put it on her desk alongside other things St. John sent from his travels to prove he hadn't died from a shoot-out or the grippe since the Gold Rush: a rock speckled with flecks of gold, a certificate for life insurance from New York, and an envelope that was always full of cash. When her children came in to see her during her morning correspondence, she would show them the things their father had sent. Her children told her to stop being so loony. "That man," they would say, "isn't my father. My father is some guy from down at the bar." And Tillie would say, "I've been to that bar once in my life. Once."

Tillie kept getting pregnant. She thought of each man as someone St. John had sent to keep her company. First, it was Laurie. Then it was a string of men and boys Laurie hired to do odds and ends, including deliver her envelope of cash every week, the profits from the bar. Often, when making love, she swore to the men she could see St. John through the window. She would stop in the middle and sit up, pointing into the darkness. He was coming through the cornfield, with his full-throated singing and the moon shining on his boots. The men would push her back into the pillows and grow rough with trying to kiss away her thoughts of him.

*

In the late afternoon, Theresa takes a bath. She needs to be at work by six. She called her boss to pick her up before he opens shop. Her car is still at the parlor. He didn't have questions, but Theresa knows there will be something coming once she gets in his truck. Her boss is not sure if Theresa has any sense. Theresa doesn't know if this should bother her, or if she should be thankful someone has noticed that she might not.

She braids her hair into one long slick down her back. She has turned out better than she expected. There is some color along her cheeks from the salt scratching. Her sleepy eyes look darkly eyeshadowed, demure. Apart from her ear, it is like nothing happened. She checks her bag to make sure she has her keys. They are there, next to the magazine the guy shoved in before they left the parlor, before he poked her in the back of the ribs and she laughed.

It is a girly magazine: women wearing yellow and red swimsuits, posing with Harleys and Ferraris. So, this is what he came back to get: leather miniskirts. Everything looks ready to pop. It makes Theresa feel sickly plain, gangle-boned. She lies belly-down across her bed, flipping through its pages like it's a medical guide. She gets up periodically and looks in her dresser mirror to adjust her braided hair, to pull at her collar or tuck the hem of her skirt tighter.

In the back, there are advertisements for cars, tanning beds, leather jackets, how-to booklets. The magazines and the booklets she ordered helped fill the great voids she had from living with Tillie. She used to send for things in these back pages when she was younger, twelve, thirteen. A mood ring, shimmering skin powders, exercise pamphlets. She didn't have a checkbook or know what a money order was, so she sent cash. Sometimes it worked, sometimes it didn't. She never got her mood ring. She is about to flip the magazine shut, when, between two of the pages, she finds a one-hundred-dollar bill. It's worn soft and taped at one end. There is fuchsia lipstick smeared across Benjamin Franklin's face that is now mostly grey and sticky with fingering. Under it is a half-page call: ACTORS WANTED—Opportunities in Hollywood, California—Extras Needed for ALL KINDS OF SCENES—All Types Wanted—Big Roles Around Every Corner!—Send $89.99 + tax, shipping, and handling for Directory of Agencies, incl. Addresses and Phone Numbers, plus FREE pamphlet: Advice From The Experts—. So, Theresa thinks, he wanted to get away, and before she even knew she loved him. It wouldn't do. Theresa has never before felt so possessive of a human being, besides Tillie, so jealous of his opportunities. She has never felt more like Tillie.

Her boss lays on his horn. Theresa stuffs the magazine and money back into her bag. She makes herself look like Theresa again. When she looks out the window, Tillie is at his truck. The summer wind is blowing steady. Tillie is wearing a little straw boating hat because her hair is still matted from sleep. She presses it down and the wind plays with what hangs from her arm—sleeve, skin, a bangle. Theresa hurries. When she gets to the truck, Tillie turns and says, "I was just telling this one that he's not the first calling for you today."

"Let's get you settled in," Theresa says, and loops her arm around Tillie's elbow. Tillie follows. She says, "But this guy is more my age."

Today is not one of Tillie's better days. It is Theresa's fault: the early wakeup, the hiding. Theresa has Tillie shake off her house slippers and then takes her all the way to the couch, as if she will stay there until Theresa comes home. Tillie sits, holding Theresa's hand until Theresa doesn't know what to do and says she has to go. On her way out, she picks up a robe and pillows, pushes in chair legs that anyone could trip over.

*

The church ladies didn't warn Tillie what day they'd be coming to interview her for the book. Two of them just came knocking one rare afternoon when Theresa was four and misbehaving. Theresa was pale with hysterics. Tillie was conked out on the dining room floor. She barely had time to wipe Theresa's face dry and change into a pantsuit—Theresa watching her swap clothes and whispering to God all the while that she'd never be bad for Tillie again. The ladies were halfway back to their LeSabre before Tillie got to the door.

It didn't take Tillie long to realize that all they wanted to see was her stained glass. She was old and likely crazy. They wouldn't be quoting her.

Tillie was famous for the glass, in certain circles, for a time. The priest, when the church was being built across from the mine in the 1940s, solicited Tillie to build windows for the vestibule. She did. Two large, arched panels with the church's saints: their faces upturned and expectant. Their brows sweating and their bodies tormented. In the background of the left panel is a cave with an angel sitting inside. The bottom reads, *Why do you look for me here?* On the right panel, a cliff runs along the far side. Palaces dot the bottom. On top of the cliff are two figures—one haloed, the other winged. The bottom reads, *All these things I will give to you. . . .*

Tillie handed the ladies a small rectangular piece, one of her earlier designs: just brown, bunchy earth and the river running along what was supposed to be the distance but was also up in the sky—her perspective, at first, was off. The surface is textured, sharp. The piece needs to be held by the edges to avoid cuts. The lead ribbons are uneven and clotted at the joints. This was accidental, but, Tillie thought, exactly how it was at first—the lead lying about the ground. Sometimes, the horseshoe nails she used to hold the glass pieces in place became melted into the lead. That was fine, too.

"It's a little ugly, isn't it?" one said.

"It's best from a distance," the other lady said, and held it out with her arm. "See?"

"Here," Tillie said, and took the piece from them. She walked it out a few feet and held it for them. She tried to catch the sunlight. She wanted to tell them a story about St. John leaving, something noble, but there wasn't one. The book would not paint him kindly. He is, to the town, another man who abandoned them. A historical figure to whom Tillie formed an attachment, through all those years of collecting lead for her work, of hearing St. John's history echoed in a town with bluffs and valleys where nothing much happens. Even in her mind, she can't justify his leaving. She had told him night after night that wherever he went, she would go. It took her weeks to realize he'd actually left. Longer to realize he might not return. Within a year, the boomtown fell to pieces. And then, it seemed like weeks later, but it couldn't have been, her eldest flew off to Chicago to sing in a nightclub. She sent a flyer home once, with a drawing of her—

"What's the best part of making stained glass?" a lady read from her notebook, and looked up, smiling.

"The only good thing about stained glass," Tillie said, "is that everything stays still."

The phone rings, and Tillie has been staring out the window since Theresa left for work. It's dark out. Tillie shakes the blood back into her feet and eases herself up. The phone is past its tenth ring by the time Tillie gets to it. The nightlight down the hall is flicking on and off, always hanging out of its socket. The sockets are too old for all this stuff.

"Theresa there?" the guy asks. He's chewing on something.

"She's at work," she says. "And you'd better be good to her." But he's already hung up.

Tillie dials the tattoo parlor, but the line is busy.

Theresa is scheduling an appointment for tomorrow night, saying goodbye, hanging up the phone. She can just hear her boss in the other room, singing to himself as he wipes down the chair, loads the equipment into the autoclave. She takes the magazine out of her bag, opens it to the page her guy has marked, and rips out the half-page call for actors. She folds the page until it fits in her wallet. If he wants to leave her, he will have to find another way. She sets the magazine and the money on the counter and waits for him to come.

Tillie hangs up the phone. She would like to grab the front of this kid's shirt and pull him to her face. Tell him that she means business and that he had better mean business, too. Theresa is it. She's all that's left.

When St. John woke to find her in the cave that first morning, he was beside himself. Her hair, she knew, had grown wild from sleeping. She'd loosened her dress. It'd grown unbearably tight. He told her he hadn't said anything to her father about a wife. He didn't know what to do, he said, and when he said it—so confused, as if she were a mystery—she felt beautiful, which had not happened before. "What if someone followed you here?" he asked. "What would they think?" She took his crisp white shirt in her fists and pulled him close to her lips, her lips just grazing his face with all the words she was saying, until he promised up and down that he was hers and that he would love her until the day he died. And for all Tillie knows, he could be dead.

If There Is Need of Blessings

She pulled the nightgown over her head, and that was her costume. Hazel was a Child of God. The nightgown was long-sleeved and lace-trimmed. Blue stripes ran up and down, with rosebuds spaced between. Her mother had picked it out a month ago in a Wal-Mart. Hazel was with her, but had nodded only that she liked it. She had not known the nightgown was for her. Her mother had taken up charity work recently, and Hazel assumed in her own vague way that it was for one of those girls, those charity cases. The nightgown had its charm. It reminded Hazel of a comfortable other time, when girls wore ribbons to bed, hoping their curls would hold the next day. Those girls might like the nightgown, Hazel thought. And then she thought of something else. That is how it is with thirteen-year-olds.

Hazel was in the girls' bathroom at the school. Her classmates were changing into their Halloween costumes. All of the eighth-grade girls—save Hazel, whose costume was easily slipped into, thoroughly uncomplicated in its own way—all seven of them were bunched in front of the two sinks, the two mirrors. The Virgin Mary looked down at them from above the paper towel dispenser. Even in the bathroom, while the youngest Steiger girl applied clotted rubber blood to her feline cheekbone, judgments were being made.

Today was the Halloween parade. Since they were eighth graders, this was the last time they would shuffle down the short hallway, do a loop around the gym, and meander through the rows of desks in each of the eight classrooms. Hazel would do this barefoot. Shoes would not do with a nightgown. Then there would be cupcakes and candy corn in each of the classrooms while the teachers prepared for parent-teacher conferences. Next year, in public high school, they would all act as though none of this happened, or as if it happened many years ago.

On Hazel's nightgown, there was a construction-paper sign that had been safety-pinned to the back. It read *Child of God.* That was what made it a costume and not just a nightgown. The safety pins created a conflict. They gave her a choice. The choice would remind her, in later years, of the time a man moved out of the house she shared with him. He left photos of himself, of them. Mementos, trinkets. Notes for her to find. And all that empty space. Hazel had left them out, though she wasn't sure how she felt about the man at the time beyond knowing she was not angry with him. Surely, she thought, you would only take down someone's photo if you never wanted to see that person again. Of course, she knew leaving the trinkets out implied something else that wasn't exactly true. It was frustrating, that he left them up for her to deal with, for her to make a statement, one way or the other. She only took them down when she left the house to move in with him again, in a new place a thousand miles away. That had felt like a completely fresh start.

Hazel left the sign on her back. She was a Child of God. That is what they do.

Missionaries would come to school that night. There would be a big church meeting in the gym. A revival is what they could have called it, if the congregation did not feel it was above being revived. Hazel's mother, Ginny, had met the missionaries at a conference somewhere across Iowa and recommended them to the priest. There were flyers put into the bulletin, announcements made at the end of Mass. Complaints were made about trick-or-treating interruptions, so there would be refreshments. It would not go well. Ginny does not know the first thing about hospitality, gift-giving, or parties. This only became more obvious as Hazel grew older. Orange Jell-O with carrot shavings and stacks of wrapped cheese slices. For Christmas, presents of frozen ground beef. The missionaries, a couple, had names too phony to mention as far as Hazel was concerned.

"Nice costume," a seventh grader told her as the parade twisted into a U outside the music room at the end of the hallway. He was a brainiac, and had enough of a crush on Hazel to assume she was being ironic. He lifted his pitchfork up the way a gentleman would a cap.

"Thank you." Hazel was not worried about her reputation. She wouldn't even know she had a reputation until she found herself drinking with classmates in a dive bar several Thanksgivings too late to manage that long-ago life.

That was not to say the costume didn't bother her. The costume was revenge. That summer, Ginny had caught Hazel with Jack, who was a wonder on the high school football field. What began as some earnest kissing twisted into Hazel demonstrating the act of speaking in tongues. This was one of her early and rare attempts to bond. She had told Jack the speaking was amazing, that she lusted for it. She had used that word, lusted. But because she was unable to relay something amazing, she had panicked and made a joke of it. She took staggering steps forward and back. She yammered with her eyes closed because that was what she had seen her mother do.

"That's so good," Jack had said. He had rubbed his watering eyes and laughed. "That's really great." He'd always had such girlish hands.

She did not know how long her mother watched her, silently and endlessly wiping her hands clean with a dish towel.

Though Hazel would never realize this, the rest of her decade-long relationship with Jack was her revenge for his laughing so long that afternoon.

The Catholic school was small, seventy-six students if no one had the flu, and the parade was mandatory. The Timmer siblings who flaunted their money were dressed as Paul Bunyan and Babe the Blue Ox, but apart from that, it was the same as last year. The packaged princess costumes from the discount stores, the Jason mask, the Freddie with its crooked rubber hands. A gaggle of diner waitresses because the whole world was tired of witches. Mr. Hues, their one male teacher, gym, tried to make jokes as they shuffled along, but he was too clever for some and too insultingly stupid for others. A ghost tripped over its own feet, which had toilet paper wrapped around them for invisibility.

*

Years later, after Jack, and after some other things that didn't pan out, Hazel finds herself in Miami with Smith. If there is one thing she can say about Smith, it is that he has a great dog.

The dog wears a muzzle for walks and barks violently at Hazel whenever she wants anything at all. Hazel's arms are etched with thin white scars from the dog's wild jumping and lunging. She and Smith often joke that no man could ever bring himself to marry her with such scars. They joke as if they aren't a couple because marriage has felt, from the first, off the table, possibly forever at their age. Smith is older than she and thinks himself incapable of almost everything.

"I can't do a pull-up anymore," he will say, panicking and coming from the bathroom where he has gone to brush his teeth. "It's hard to even hold the toothbrush," he says, and nearly drops it. Smith has an electric toothbrush. He bought the best.

Smith works in government regulations and spends a lot of time alone in his office, thinking about how he does not like this co-worker who had, out of the blue, given him a small cactus to care for. The cactus was thriving. Hazel is in arts administration, but only part-time, and feels as though her real job is walking the dog. Walking the dog is not only taxing but also how she builds her reputation: The Lady with the Bad Dog. She and Smith do not go out often because Smith, who is normally docile, transforms in traffic, and Hazel is compelled to holler. This has led to several close calls. They are only leasing the Corolla. They walk almost everywhere, even to work and to get groceries. "You'll have to carry the bags," Smith says. "My arms are giving out. Feel them. Just feel this muscle right here."

Smith's other co-worker, Jed, who is slightly younger, and who Smith enjoys for his good business sense, owns rental property in several states and suggested to Smith that they all go out to a mall for Halloween.

"Only in Miami," Hazel says, "would people go to a mall for Halloween."

"It's a thing," Smith says. "It's a thing people do here."

"A Miami thing."

"South Beach."

Hazel rolls her eyes and walks away, though not far. The apartment is painfully small. She has been roundly ignoring Halloween for the past twenty years. Jack would do whatever she asked, and she often begged off from going to parties on account of work or illness. Neither entirely untrue, she was often busy or sick. Hazel hates feigning merriment, and that is what a costume implies: merriment and playfulness.

Hazel and her mother last spoke over a year ago. During the conversation, Ginny mentioned that she was getting a perm the next week. At the time, Hazel had been considering moving closer to home, *to be there,* and all the things that phrase implied. No one was getting younger. But the thought of her mother with a perm threw Hazel into a panic. Ginny had had them in the past, and each one created the impression that her mother's face was nothing but an eraser's smudge—hazy. "And now, when you know I'm moving home," Hazel had said, as though the perm was yet another form of revenge, meant to show the daughter that she, too, would be left behind, forgettable.

"It actually looks nice. Good, even," her sister, Liz, later said over the phone. Liz did not understand Hazel's moods, especially regarding their mother, but was amused by them, and so they stayed close.

Hazel moved to Miami. She let everyone know after the fact. "Of all the things you have to worry about," Liz had said, "our mother's hair need not be one of them."

*

Thirteen-year-old Hazel wore the sign on her back when Ginny pulled the Corsica into the school parking lot. Proof to her mother that she had worn it with no shame. The October wind blew at the nightgown's skirt, and Hazel hoped she looked dramatic enough to satisfy, that her mother was pleased with the spectacle. Hazel was Ginny's last chance to raise a Christian, or so she yelled after Hazel while Hazel ran upstairs, away from some argument.

The car slowed, and Hazel shouldered her backpack to reach for the door. She stumbled on her bootlaces, which were undone, the boots slipped into right before the bell rang. She fell against the door, and in Hazel's place there was a woman in a purple jacket with gold piping. The missionaries were early. Paula rolled the window down. "*This* is the daughter?" she asked. She reached out and pulled Hazel in for a hug. The Corsica would always reek of Ginny's smoke. Not even Paula's perfume could change a thing about that.

"What a blessing," Paula said, and patted Hazel's forearm. Being called a blessing and a help has always stoked an otherwise unknown rage inside Hazel. She would be called these things for the rest of her life.

Ginny pulled away and parked the car in front of the flagpole. "But I thought we were going home," Hazel said once her mother got out. She immediately regretted speaking: Ginny had tricked her into complaining. It meant a new, more complex suffering would follow. Martin, the other missionary, stood from the backseat. He had a mustache that lifted up and out at the corners like an old broom. She turned from him, and wanted badly for the night to be finished.

Martin put his hand on her back and eased her forward. "Child of God," he read.

"It's Halloween," Hazel said.

"But this is no costume. One look at you and I can see it's no costume."

Inside, the teachers called to one another from their rooms, lingered in doorways. Completely different people from ten minutes ago. They stayed out of Ginny's way for fear of being included. They wanted to go home to Dubuque or Fennimore and order takeout—perhaps the one way their lives were superior to those of their students.

It is incredibly stupid, Hazel thought, being the only person in costume. Her brother Mark had called only last week. He said that he wouldn't be calling anymore. He thought their mother had gone berserk, and that was not lost on Hazel then, as she walked the hallway in that cheap, childish nightgown and felt pitied. The scene at Mark's wedding had been too much, and he had a wife to think of, loyalties. Hazel had said she would pass the message along. But she hadn't, and she wouldn't. It was her secret: that she too could break away, fall off the map. Not have a thing to do with any of it. But still, she wanted it. That thorn in her heart.

She followed Martin to the gymnasium. He opened a suitcase on the gym floor. Leaned the lid against the bleachers. Everything was packed tidily. The clothes rolled, military-style. He took out a short stack of books to sell—*Spiritual Warfare, Speaking with The Spirit,* and a plastic bag with many different jars and tubs of holy oils and balms. They were for the blessings, if there was need of them. Hazel dropped her backpack and the sound echoed through the gym.

"What do you have in there, a brick?"

Hazel shook her head. "Nothing." Martin brought her bag to his lap and smiled at her. Only boys her own age had smiled at her this way: Jack, before he took her under the arms and spun her, squealing, onto a couch. Before Hazel could take it from him, Martin had unzipped the backpack. He looked: folders, romance novels, bundled clothes she changed out of before the parade. He took her clothes, stuck his hands in the pockets, the neckline, turned them outside in, folded them. What did it matter? This man was versed in the whole family, and had made judgments about each of them: her father's unbelief, the children's failures, Ginny's wild desire for another, better, child. Her mother had asked for his prayers regarding Hazel and her betrayals to the faith. It was a violation, Hazel thought: this man had prayed about her most intimate desires. He had contemplated her parents in bed.

"Give me your boots," Martin said, and held out his hand. "I'll pack them on the bottom. Next to your Harlequins." He winked.

"I'll just take my clothes," Hazel said, and bent to take the folded stack from the bleacher. She was cold in the nightgown and after looking through the glass gym doors, she realized the nightgown was see-through, which seemed impossible while it hung in all its innocence from that rack in a Wal-Mart.

Martin placed his hand on top of her balled socks. "But you've kept your robe on this long. No." He paused, then went on as if he was confused, "No, this must be like those years you prayed for the stigmata."

Ginny had told him everything.

"And why was that?" Martin asked. He listed the reasons off on his fingers, his voice childish. "So it would be easier, so that people knew, so they understood your great faith, no need to ask questions." He took her hand and looked at it as if it were the most precious thing he'd seen, stroked the back with both thumbs. "So young," he murmured, "such zeal," and seemed about to bring it to his face. "No," he said again, "you can't change. There isn't a thing more blessed than you walking around." Then Paula was behind her, her hand on Hazel's shoulder. Her earrings clattered like some dog's tags. If only someone would put a stop to this, Hazel thought. The missionaries stood there with their hands on her. She bent and took off her boots. Martin zipped them into her bag. It would be many years before she realized she could put a stop to anything at all.

*

They end up going to the mall on South Beach. Halloween is on a Friday, and Hazel fought it all afternoon, right up until they left.

"Go—just go without me. It will be good for you," she had said.

"I can't go alone," Smith said. "I can't handle Jed by myself. He'll want to talk about titties and ass. And money. He'll make me feel bad about the way I spend my money." Smith had just bought a one-hundred-dollar hamstring stretcher that he'd overheard his co-worker recommending in the hall. This was the co-worker who had given him the cactus. Hazel believes Smith is having a crisis, or perhaps a breakdown, and feels certain she will move before the year is through.

She goes because Jed is intense and will make Smith drink more than he can handle. Smith can never resist an evening's momentum. They are only leasing the Corolla.

It is an outdoor mall, straight up and down for blocks. Because it is difficult to find parking, they park outside a luxury grocer and walk a ways, across the causeway and past some seedy apartments, to get there. This puts Smith in a bad mood, and he mumbles the whole walk, past revelers and drunks, about how she has failed to find a reason for them to cancel.

Hazel likes to imagine he is joking when he does this, and so she ignores him.

She had not bothered to change after work. "We're too old for this," she says. Her slacks bag and whip around her legs.

The bar is known for its beer and has a monastic theme. None of this is obvious at first. A man on a stool near the entrance is dressed as an STD. The woman with him has a large net, and periodically catches him. Jed is not there yet.

"Let's say we got the wrong place. Let's go. We can get sandwiches."

Smith is too depressed to make a decision, and so he sits at the bar and starts a tab, which is what the bartender suggests.

Hazel sips. While they wait at the bar, three men approach her at different times. They each have a short conversation with her. One tells her she is no fun. The second asks who she thinks she's supposed to be with those pants on. The third asks if she is ready to go home, and she says yes, which catches him off guard and he backs away. It is too early for that kind of talk. Smith flexes his hands along the bar top, to see which side of his body is failing him.

She is glad when Jed appears. Smith can put on an act when he wants to, and Hazel appreciates the effort. She cannot stand Smith's friends and dreads the thought of entertaining them on her own. She is certain they think she is a failure. She makes so little money.

"Teri called," Jed says, and shakes Smith's hand. "She's at a bachelorette party. Weepy, at a bachelorette party." It is an apology for being late. Hazel has not met Teri, but she imagines Jed's girlfriend is very young and a little stupid. But that might just be Jed. He has the deep, raspy voice of someone who might be stupid.

"She wanted a couple's costume. So—" Jed lifts his arms and turns around. He looks normal for him, which is not to say normal. His eyes often seem as though they are popping out of his head—the result, Hazel thinks, of what he would call too much "ab strength."

He is religious about the gym and counts reps while chewing gum, if his jawline is any indication. "I dyed the armpits myself," he says.

They're dressed as an unhappily married couple from a '90s sitcom. Teri, weeping with envy at some strip club on the outskirts of the city, wears leopard print and carries bonbons. "It's perfect," Jed says. "She's Peg, so she can be, you know, sexual. Women like that, looking sexual."

"And you can drink," Hazel says, "and sit on the couch." Men with dumb girlfriends love flirting with women who call them out, especially if the women are slightly older.

"And I can drink."

They move to a booth. Each time Hazel gathers at a table, she feels someone must pray and that it not be her. Anxiety more than habit, as she has rarely been a table-eater with anyone, let alone the prayerful. Once a month at most, when Liz first brought a boyfriend home, and it had seemed right to set an example. And now Liz was married to this boyfriend and happy and liked their mother's perm. Occasionally, it all works out.

The one time their brother Mark visited town with his then-fiancée, he sent place settings along ahead of time: a set of plates, a set of silverware. Three bottles of excellent wine. He enclosed a note for Ginny, telling her to buy napkins. Ginny didn't unpack the plates. They sat in their boxes in the corner by the doorway. Hazel's father unknowingly began to set his work boots on the box when he came in from chores. When Mark arrived with his fiancée, they all went out to eat at the supper club. Ginny said a very long grace before the meal came out. A fly got caught in the cheese spread on the relish tray. Hazel watched it try to get out. Her mother was trying to prove something by praying so long. The regulars at the bar were staring. It was Hawaiian night, and the drink special was Sex on the Beach. The bartender had given their father a Buttery Nipple. Ginny made up the couch for Mark's fiancée, but they didn't stay the night. Mark made getting out look much easier than it was. "Just leave," he would say, "come stay with us," and in a heartbeat he'd be doing something else, buttering a biscuit as though they'd been talking about football.

"What you need," Jed tells Smith, "is for Hazel to get a new job. She's still marketable. Then you could buy your apartment within a year. That'd be a leg up." Jed has both a double and a beer in front of him, his second of both. Jed is serious in all things. Smith sits up straight in the booth next to him, eyes focused well past Hazel. The money fears have him assessing the disc he believes has slipped in his lower back. That or the tumor he feels above his kneecap.

"You could be a bartender. They rake it in compared to you." So they'd talked about her and her failures. That must have happened during some titties and ass happy-hour conversation she wasn't privy to.

"You're not too old, either," Jed said. "I know what you're going to say—you're easy to read. You know you can still make good tips at your age. Look at you."

"But I have these arms," Hazel says, ponying to control the mood. She holds her forearms out to show him the scars from the dog, but the lighting is bad and the scars are hard to see.

A cowboy comes up to the booth and slides four dripping shots of bourbon onto the table. They sit there in a puddle until the cowboy shouts a toast in some other language, and they drink.

*

When Hazel was that girl who wore the pinstripe nightgown, the girl who made lists of her favorite movies, the handsome actors, she did not imagine nights like this—or, no, she imagined nights like this, but assumed she would enjoy them. When she grew up, she believed she would have children, or that perhaps she would walk along a city street in a black suit carrying a briefcase, doing something mysterious yet pressing. She did not imagine that the overgrown revelry, the exposition, of a night out would be so similar to the nights spent at revivals in church basements, gyms—events that happened off the grid, sanctioned by nobody, where strangers held hands and shouted and danced. She did not imagine she could feel so separate from both of those worlds—from one or the other, perhaps, but certainly not both. Instead, these situations are the source of Hazel's unfortunate habit of waiting for every stage in her life to be over.

At the bar's exit, there is a man dancing on the boardwalk. There are drums strapped to him so he can dance to the beat he sets. A mass has gathered around him because he is fast and muscled. He has no shirt on. The mall has foot traffic pushing both ways. Hazel holds her purse close to her, certain the strap will break and that her few things will be vomited on, trampled. She calls back to Smith. There is an alley up ahead that should open out, onto an emptier street.

"We're back here," Jed says. He takes her arm. "You can't get away so easily. This punch is supposed to be toxic." He is guiding her back, past the drummer whose crowd is drifting with him, down the mall, like he's the pied piper. Jed brings her to a drink cart. Smith comes from behind, holding three yellow cups in a triangle, all the cups splashing from his outspread elbows being run into. His front is wet with red.

"I don't want one," Hazel says.

Jed hands one to her. "Come on," he says. "You're sexy. Stop acting like you're not."

Jed drinks. "I could use a smoke."

"I didn't know you smoked," Smith says. He finds lung disease astonishing and holds deep breaths regularly to avoid it. He has Hazel time him for worrisome deviations.

"Don't worry," Hazel says, and she leaves them. Anything to leave. She fishes a dollar from her purse and bunches it into her back pocket.

In the gym that night, Martin had instructed Hazel to sit in front of the bleachers, on a chair near him. Hazel had hoped no one would come. But they did show—not for Ginny or the missionaries, but for the priest. The priest was taken seriously. Even her Jack with his girlish, footballer hands showed, because he was in love.

After Martin and Paula spoke their usual, they passed a collection basket around. To support their travels, their work. The many pious families, the plumbers, the hairdressers, the concrete dealer and his wife—and all with their children—threw in crumbled dollars, fives. Some had checks prepared. The children were costumed, but the costumes were barely visible. They'd been bundled against the October chill. Just a pirate's eye patch, or a zebra's mane of yarn sneaking out from a bunched scarf. No one (save Jack, who wore a sweater with a plastic knife sunk into the chest, latex blood exploding) was certain Halloween could be safely celebrated at something like a church service. The costumes would be shown off later, in the parking lot, before the children went door to door. Once the crowd showed, Hazel prayed Martin would leave her alone, that the nightgown was no longer see-through, that Martin would say something offensive, go long, or otherwise drive them out before it was over. Hazel shivered, her bare feet crossed one over the other, and sat across from her mother. Ginny twisted in her seat and looked out at the crowd. Full bleachers. She smiled at Hazel and whispered something to her that Hazel could not hear.

Hazel dumps her drink in the trash and spots a mafioso smoking on the corner. She takes the dollar from her pocket. It's dark and crumpled. Only a desperate person would take it. She asks if she can buy a cigarette off him.

"Honey, you need never pay me." He shakes one out. He keeps them in a case with a diamond latch. She inhales and makes her way back to the drink cart with the cigarette held in the air.

"Here you go." She puts it in Jed's hand. He is talking to some girl with a tapered waist and a belly ring.

"Where's your drink?"

"Pounded it."

"Liar."

"Did you smoke that?" Smith asks.

The shirtless drummer taps her on her shoulder. "Can I kiss you?" Before she can say a thing, he has kissed her. "Magic," he says, and Hazel turns away.

"I hardly know you," Smith whines. "You don't smoke."

"Let's go." She takes Smith's hand and pulls him toward the alley she had gone toward minutes ago. He is drunk, and is exaggerating the force of each person he runs into. He has his own methods of charm.

Around the corner, into the alley, there is a DJ set up. He is one of several along the mall. There is a short metal gate, just beyond his gear, that blocks off the alley. Teenagers jump over the gate and security catches some of them, only to help them climb back over. Dancers pool in and forget they were trying to leave.

"Whoa, whoa, whoa," Jed says. He hands Smith another cup and then stands between the two of them. "It's too early." She didn't think he had followed them. The woman he had been talking with stood behind him, waiting. "Dance with me," Jed says. He takes Hazel's hand and holds it above their heads. He shakes his hips girlishly and waits for her to move. "C'mon," he says. He takes her by the hips, his fingers in the loops of her pants, then over the edge of her waistline. He tries to move her the way he wants her to move. The woman behind him has left.

"What is this?" Hazel asks. She feels a million miles away.

"You have a real chip on your shoulder," Jed says. The music is thumping in and out. Someone with a stupid, last-minute top-hat costume looks over at them. "You know, you're damaged goods. Women like you drive men insane. Look at him. Look what you've done." Jed points over to the speakers. Smith is doubled over, vomiting into a puddle. He holds his stomach gently like he's had too much gravy at dinner. "He's ruined."

Hazel goes to Smith. She wipes his lips with her shirt and stands there with him. A group of young Scottish tourists gathers around. They want to know if this is what every weekend is like, or if they've only picked a good one. Jed goes from woman to girl. He has three he likes the best, and he trails them. "What about Teri?" Smith shouts. "What about your girlfriend?

Smith asks again, while they walk to the car, "What about Teri?" Hazel holds Smith under his shoulder. Jed trips on the curb and falls down. "I'm going to marry her," he says. "But then I'm going to marry them." He pulls himself up and leans against the parking meter. "I'm going to marry them all," he says, and makes to stand up. "I am the Great Uniter, Smith. Take note." Hazel tucks Smith into the passenger seat. She walks around the car, gets in, and starts it. "But what about Jed?" Smith asks. "He's wild about you."

*

After the money basket had passed through the bleachers, Ginny collected it and brought it to the table, where Martin had gestured. Paula sat in the corner opposite Hazel and played her guitar just enough to calm the crowd, to open the moment. Martin prayed. He opened with words of thanksgiving and forgiveness—he offered praise. He moved on and asked the congregation for petitions. Together, they prayed for a grandmother, a hip surgery, a benign tumor, a baby with colic, a nephew with leukemia. He pressed them harder. He asked them to come forward, to profess. They did not. Weariness had set in. It had been a full hour. Jack leaned his elbow against the bleachers, and his knife bunched up under his armpit. The fluorescent lamps overhead flickered and hummed. A woman replaced a coffee urn on the refreshment table and rearranged the frosted pumpkin cut-outs. Martin stepped closer to the bleachers. He paced and spoke of the lack of faith he had found in this town. "Faith requires a fight," he said. "Do you have the scars of faith?" They nodded. A couple adjusted a red stocking cap on their toddler's head and made their way down the bleachers, slumping as though they could hide their leaving. It was after seven. It was taking longer than they had thought. They would nod when he wanted them to, if it meant they could go.

"I know of a girl," he put his hand on Hazel's shoulder, "who would pray for God to mark her, all so you would know. So you faithless would know." Jack came to, as though it were about to get good. He nodded at Hazel and smiled. Martin pulled Hazel up from her chair and turned her around. He read the back of her sign to them: "Child of God." He said it again, slowly. Hazel was sure Martin would not have done or said these things if he had thought them through. If he felt he had done well that night, if the crowd had responded, or given more money. She, too, has spoken in the heat of the moment, has continued to speak and even to defend things she did not believe because there was an audience and there was pride. The rule is to never back down in front of an audience.

He began to pray that she would receive the scars. He had them pray along with him. Hazel, still turned, heard them mumbling, repeating the words he said. They did not care. If there was anything, it was resentment: she was taking their time by being his example. He said that she alone could turn these lost hearts back around. Hazel had often prayed for a loss of control with regard to her faith. She regularly felt rigid and inhospitable, and would pray to be softened, to be overtaken, overwhelmed. This was not that—this was not a prayer answered. Or could it be that twisted, serpentine answer, the utter denial? No, it was not even that. From where she stood, the gym was completely empty; everything was behind her. She could trace the lines of the basketball court, study the blank scoreboard. It was relaxing, if she let it be. She could hear more feet making their way down the wooden, creaking bleachers.

Martin took Hazel by the shoulders and turned her around. The congregation was halved, winnowed. Many of the mothers left had purse straps or diaper bags shouldered. The insurance salesman in the first row tapped his wallet on his knee, waiting to slide it into his back pocket once he stood. Jack unwrapped a stick of gum. He would kiss her, after, and he was vain about his mouth.

Hazel heard the clinking of the glass lid and saw the jar of fragrant oil. It was the size of a sparrow and made of cut green glass. Martin cupped it in one hand. He let the lid flip from his hands as he spoke, and Hazel was sure it was an accident. He did not flinch. It broke neatly in two pieces near his feet. Righteous anger, Ginny would later say.

Martin dipped his thumb in the oil and walked back to Hazel. She had not finished looking at the broken lid. He took his index finger and raised her chin, stroked her neck with the back of his finger as though she were a songbird. His breath was sugary, and there were crumbles of cookie at the outer edges of his mustache. "I anoint you," he said, and ran his thumb down the center of her forehead. He dipped once more and ran his thumb across her temple. He left her, and Hazel let her chin fall. Martin encouraged them all, "once more," he said, to profess. A drop of oil ran down the bridge of Hazel's nose. The plumber's wife yawned and unwrapped a butterscotch to give to her son, who had a dry cough. Martin held the jar in both hands and let it drop. It did not break so neatly as the lid. Shards of green glass spread out across the gym floor, and the oil spread to Hazel's feet, the chair legs. It was only a small jar, but it was enough to keep Hazel from moving. She had dealt with broken glass before. The slivers were impossible to find, to dig out, once they'd gotten in the skin.

After the glass had broken, Martin let the congregation out, row by row, to meet Hazel, the way an usher releases guests out of a wedding ceremony to meet the happy couple. He motioned for Ginny to give Hazel a pot of balm, and so she brought a tin-lidded thing. Hazel's mother had platinum hair that waved to her shoulders then, and she looked as she had in her honeymoon photos: fiery-eyed, dramatically beautiful. "Use your thumb," Ginny said, "just the side of it, like this. It will come to you."

"Be blessed," Martin said to the parishioners as they filed past him. "Go and be blessed."

The families walked down the bleachers and out the gym door. Unaware, Hazel was sure, of what was happening, what they were supposed to do. Jack came up to her with his hands clasped as the congregation passed behind him. Already, they were chatting about their evening's rounds. Some sang along to Paula's guitar, a common hymn about fellowship flowing like a river. Green glass crackled beneath Jack's sneakers, and she was afraid he might slip on the holy oil.

"Is this it?" Jack whispered. He looked around, excited. His heart a rubbery red burst. "Is this what you've been waiting for?"

So Very Nice

Every family pitches in for the parish fall festival. John and Edna Sweeney, childless, bring homemade candies and plastic kites and jack-and-ball sets for the Yum-Yum Tree. Laura and Kevin Lang bring, along with Kevin Jr., napkins, Kleenex, and wet-wipes. They distribute them liberally—at the ring toss, the cakewalk, the tables where a turkey dinner is served. They don't let little Kevin near the Yum-Yum Tree, as it is filled with choking hazards. Each member of the Knights of Columbus buys a keg for the beer tent—28 kegs in all. Hazel, twelve, brings a bag of Harlequin romance novels for the book sale. She knows she will leave with another full bag. The book sale doesn't draw a crowd, and they start giving the books away. Hazel's mother, Ginny, has her jeans pocket stuffed with religious tracts. She is trying to convert Father Beschler. Hazel's father has brought a piglet. Later, if the parish raises enough money—$2000—for renovations, Father Beschler has promised to kiss the pig. Jack's parents, though they don't attend, donate a set of golf clubs that will be given to the putt-putt competition winner. They are sure Jack will win. He doesn't go to lessons for nothing. Tillie, who is not right in the head, throws together two pies with lattice crusts for the dinner. Instead of baking powder and raisins, she uses drain cleaner and chocolates. She cuts her thumb twice with her paring knife while peeling apples. These are the mistakes you make when you're in a hurry. When Alberta, a church biddy, comes to pick up Tillie, the pies aren't baked, and Theresa, Tillie's eight-year-old granddaughter, is placing a Band-Aid on Tillie's thumb. Theresa's wool pants hit her mid-calf.

Father Beschler has brought himself and all his infinite wisdom. The festival is held at the grade school, and the priest paces up and down the one short hallway. Most of the games are down in the gymnasium. Up here, there is only the cakewalk and an arts and crafts room. Still, there are interruptions—pats on the back, requests for prayers—that he deals with in turn. He drums his fingers on his chest as if his heart is a piano, which, in fact, he once used to think: its many strings and keys, the rich tones. *The heart is a piano.* He can remember saying this in sermons when he had a different parish, and to friends over supper while making a toast. He is considering this morning's sermon, and how he quoted *Reader's Digest* once again. He made several comments about harvesting but failed to explain the metaphors. He did not think they would understand. Unless, perhaps, he turned it into a parlor game—*A farmer is to God as a harvest is to* ______. Father Beschler believes the scripted parts should do the trick. The Hail Marys, et cetera, should get them into heaven fine. His sermons are short and easily understood, though rarely relevant. The congregation loves him. Love is a virtue. He nods and his nod looks like a tremor.

The hallways are decorated with heavy black bunting. In the corners and along the edges are gauzy cotton spider webs with latex spiders perched in them. Each time the school doors open, the breeze makes the webs dance. The spiders jump. There is a scarecrow at one end of the hallway, on top of several straw bales. If this year is like every other of Father Beschler's twenty stationed here, a man dressed like the scarecrow will take the scarecrow's place at intervals and jump to frighten the children. It is terrifying to hear those screams. Only a child, Father thinks, could enjoy this festival. They have no real fear.

Bobbie Richards, three years old and crowned with ringlets, climbs into the scarecrow's lap and shakes the mini Etch-A-Sketch.

She has just won it at the fish pond. "It doesn't do anything," she tells the priest, and holds it out to him.

"It's usually harder than it looks," he says. He does not want to step any closer to the scarecrow.

*

Ginny is out to find the priest, but she just keeps running into her husband, or the Pig Man, as the congregation has taken to calling him today. A group from the beer tent even thought to fashion a little crown out of braided cornhusks and set it on his flat head. "Without you," they said as they crowned him, "we wouldn't have any of this." Two of the men curtsied. Frank could not tell if they were mocking him or if this was sincere drunken admiration. The thought terrified him: what an idea—having the priest kiss a pig. He remembered a joke about a beautiful woman and an ugly millionaire at a bar: *If the price is right. . . .* The punchline is that the woman is a whore and doesn't know it. Who laughs at that kind of joke? He shook his head to get rid of it all. If God doesn't damn him, surely his wife will. In her own way, she already has. Maybe they pinned the idea on him because he brought the pig. He was working the raffle booth when Ginny saw the crown. He was taking their money: counting it, tallying it, folding it, and shoving it into a slot cut out from the top of a plastic ice cream tub. For lack of anything else to say, he shook the tub and said, "About seven hundred left to go." So solemnly!—Ginny thought, like he's burdened. And with a crown on his head. Ginny stared at him until he blushed and took it off.

The school is only so big. The priest must be hiding from her. Today, Ginny feels like a tornado. Like all the winds—holy and unholy—have blown her up into an incredible force. The priest is afraid of her, which is a good sign. Fear is progress. Fear could inspire something. This morning's sermon settled on the congregation like a mold. Ginny believed she could see it, almost, growing green on the tops of shoulder pads and dandruffed comb-overs. Ginny has an active imagination. She likes to amuse herself because, really, no one else does these days. They are all in their own worlds—Frank's

World, Planet Hazel. This morning, Ginny sat in the back of the church, like always, and on the end of the pew so she could pop her head into the aisle to make sure that Father Beschler saw her. She mouthed words at him if she had to, if he'd gotten something wrong. Ginny might be in her fifties, but she is pretty, and so she allows herself these extravagant behaviors. Prettiness covers a multitude.

Ginny has not spoken to her husband for two weeks. Hazel has been relaying messages between them, running up and down the stairs, out to the backyard, the barn. Ginny has twice caught Hazel fabricating messages in a high romantic diction, messages to meet Frank outside at midnight, underneath the old weeping willow. There they can lay their sorrows to rest, et cetera.

"This is all a joke to you?" Ginny asked her. "You think this is funny?"

Hazel shrugged. "It's starting to feel like a soap opera."

Two weeks ago, Frank the Pig Man fell out of a tree. His brother was with him. They were drunk, drunk, drunk. Ginny doesn't know how they got to the hospital. She didn't ask. She's not talking to the brother, either. Frank stayed in the hospital for one night. Then she brought him home. He stayed in bed and Hazel nursed him through some mild amnesia. Ginny was not amused, and hardly listened to Hazel's daily reports on how he was healing.

All Hazel wants is for her parents to kiss passionately, as she is sure they did at one point. She's slouched into a bench in the gymnasium, watching both of her parents glare at each other. There is a cherry ring-pop on her finger. Her lips are a wet, brilliant red. She wears a gigantic sweater, shorts, and high socks. It is too cold for wearing shorts, as her mother pointed out. They had a short, intense fight about it this morning. But Hazel has just discovered her legs. Her thighs have grown plump. This terrified her at first—she has heard about people getting fat, how easy it is. Now, though, she feels like a pure woman. Jack sits next to her, his torso turned to her and not the gym. Hazel soaks him in, his gaze, like she's a flower and he's water. *Women grow by men*—she read that in English class. But she doesn't pay any attention to him. She's sure she'll marry him someday. A kid walks by balancing four boxed cakes he's won from the cakewalk. He can't see where he's going and knocks over a toddler who cries and cries. The priest slips into the men's room behind Ginny's back. The eleven tables where Hazel eats lunch each day are covered with white paper cloths and orange streamers. Small pumpkins and a few other gourds Hazel doesn't know the names of run along the length of each. Hazel's stomach turns. Her mom was right. She should eat some real food soon, and not fill up on sugar. She stops licking her ring-pop. Finally, she asks Jack, "Has everything ever gone nuts in your house?"

Jack says, "We have a housekeeper. She takes care of all that."

The tarps they throw on the gym floor smell like petroleum and dust. Ginny takes a seat at the pie table and tries to think of something terrible to say about the tarps to Alberta, the pie lady. Alberta is responsive and kindhearted. Ginny has grown lonely in all her running around. She would like to spit out an ugly little observation and get some sympathy. But she loves the smell of the tarps and the way it hangs thick in the air with the smells of turkey and gravy. Lotto tickets, the cardboard rows of cherries and lemons showing behind their curled tabs, scatter the tarps, along with candy corn and Dum Dum wrappers, like they're in a saloon, not a school. Plastic rings plink off milk bottles. Dollar bills and tokens get slapped onto the makeshift wooden counters. A golf ball is tap-tapped along the strip of plastic grass. Three girls in pink leggings skip in a line, holding hands. It is Ginny's favorite day of the year and she will have the pecan pie, please, Alberta.

After Alberta dishes up Ginny's pie with whipped cream and a cup of coffee—which Ginny doesn't need, she's wound up so tight it looks like her eyes could pop—she goes back to the kitchen and puts the pies Tillie brought in the oven. They look fine, and they've been fine every other year. Some of the best, really, especially the apple. Tillie does something special with chives, or maybe thyme. The pies are savory and not too sweet. These old women—and Alberta's getting to be one herself—they lose everything else before they forget how to bake. Alberta remembers her own grandmother going downhill, how she would bake the most delicious monkey bread, thickly frosted and dotted with cranberries, and then, after Alberta had stuffed herself with it, her grandmother would try to brush Alberta's teeth with a potato scrubber. Her grandmother didn't want them to rot out. Alberta only fought her off by screaming for her mother.

Alberta looks out into the lunchroom, and there's Tillie sitting at the end of a table, underneath the statue of Mary mounted on the wall. She's pulled Theresa onto her withered lap and is trying to feed her. The eight-year-old's face is flushed red. Her legs must be cold with those pants she's outgrown. They are bunched and too tight around her crotch. Poor girl. Alberta makes a note to find some clothes and drop off a bag—some sweaters, some socks—just enough to get through the winter. Theresa will probably be with Tillie at least through the winter. The truth is, nobody knows what to do: leave Theresa with her grandmother or take her away and place her somewhere else, somewhere that, they've heard, might be worse? And even if they thought it best to do just that, they wouldn't know where to start.

Tillie's hand shakes too much. It is impossible for Theresa to go along with this, and she *is* trying to go along with this, to get it over with, to stop a scene from starting. It is too easy to start a scene with Tillie these days: in the house, she is fine. But in the store, at church, there is no telling what will happen—she might pinch Theresa hard on the arm, or yell at her for talking or not talking. On Tillie's fork is a little piece of turkey that's been dipped in mashed potatoes and gravy. Tillie squeezes Theresa's side harder and harder until Theresa opens her mouth and closes her eyes. *Theresa's getting a big surprise!*—Tillie sings softly. But the food doesn't come. Tillie has started to talk to someone, the fork held midair. Theresa opens her eyes and it is her third-grade teacher, Mrs. Jennings. Mrs. Jennings is young and her bangs are always curled prettily up, away from her face. Friday, she held Theresa back after class: "I'm worried about you," she said. "Is everything okay?" Theresa nodded politely and then sprinted out the classroom door, making for the bus. Her school sack bounced against her legs, and she hoped the twine handle wouldn't break again. If she missed the bus, she'd be toast.

Theresa dangles her feet down until they reach the ground between Tillie's bony legs. If it is possible to sneak away right in front of two people, she will do it. She wills herself to be invisible. She often does this and is often disappointed to find herself, as always, horribly visible, terribly seen. Theresa takes no more than a step before Tillie shouts that she's not to take one more. "You haven't had a bite of food," Tillie says, now playfully, more to Mrs. Jennings than Theresa. "Get back here, girl."

So, Theresa sits back up on her grandmother's thigh, and Tillie shakes the forkful of food into Theresa's mouth. Gravy drips everywhere. Kids from school are staring, but not too much. They are used to Theresa's weirdness.

Tillie doesn't know why Theresa is being obstinate. She doesn't know why everyone is staring at them today. Tillie keeps coming to these festivals—the fish fries, the craft fairs, the pancake breakfasts—because she feels it's her duty. But she can't escape feeling judged. And now Theresa's teacher is here, and Theresa isn't listening. Theresa should know they need to put on a good show. Let me mother you, Tillie thinks, or else they might take you away. No one has told her this, but she can feel the hands hidden behind backs, ready to bolt and grab the one person she has left. She gives Theresa another bite, careful that the bite is not too big. "I'm sorry," Tillie says to Mrs. Jennings, "what were you saying?"

Father Beschler wonders what to do with the insane. He watches Tillie rocking Theresa in her lap, petting her arm, feeding her bites of biscuit. Theresa sitting rigid as a marionette. He has not read enough on the topic of insanity. As he looks around him, he realizes he should read more. God created the world in His image. In the same way, a priest creates a congregation in his image. On walls throughout the school are fundraising signs that read *Father Puckers for the Pig!* The men in the gym are gambling money no one has, playing blackjack—their children are tugging at shirtsleeves, begging for dollars, for candy, for more. It smells like hospital food. There is a nymphet walking around with neon lips. The beer tent is outside. Every time the gym door swings open, a raucous of catcalls and off-color punchlines and the pig's squealing comes tumbling in with the wind. Down the hall, there is screaming, over and over again—from the scarecrow trap, he hopes, but he doesn't want to find out. This scene, *this,* must be a reflection of his inner life. A pastoral Hieronymus Bosch. He studied the Dutch masters long ago. He also studied in Rome, at the Vatican. He knows philosophy and music. Still, he has created this. And now Ginny is coming up behind him. She will say to him, *Come on—let's tip over the money-grabbing tables.* She will say, *You're leading them astray.* How does he tell her he doesn't need her, that his conscience is bad enough as it is? She will not believe him. His heart was once a piano. Now, it is a kettledrum. It is the scherzo of Beethoven's Ninth Symphony: a call and response, but to whom?

Frank sits behind the raffle booth and watches his wife stalk the priest. He wishes she wouldn't go on like this, carrying her little pile of booklets around. It puts Frank in a position. People have started to tiptoe around him, or pity him. He feels like an abandoned pet they've picked up. And now, to please them, he works extra hours at the raffle booth. He keeps all the figures in a neat column. They need only five hundred dollars more before the priest will pucker up. Every hour he shouts the number out across the gym. Everyone turns and cheers. People nearby rush over to throw in some bucks. If he were to take the ice cream bucket into the beer tent, if he were to tell a few jokes and buy a few rounds, he could get that money in an hour or two. But he won't go to the beer tent. What if Ginny saw him there?

Ginny believes in the Holy Spirit. She believes people need to get rid of the junk inside to make room for the Spirit. When they talk about it, she says, *Just let go, Frank.* And if he doesn't say anything that makes her happy, she says, *What? You think you can take your cows with you when you go?* And she laughs. Frank avoids talking about it. He lets his ear hair grow.

Frank isn't filled with the Spirit. He's not filled with this family either, not usually. There are full workdays he's forgotten they had Hazel. Sometimes when he's traveling, he takes the wrong turn, the road to his childhood home, or to his first bachelor apartment. He's filled with another time, with another set of people. Two weeks ago, when he fell out of the tree, he and his brother had just finished fitting their mother with a set of dentures. They picked up the finished set from the dentist and, at the nursing home, slid them in. They asked, *How do they feel, Ma?* The brothers assumed they felt fine. She hasn't chewed food in three years.

It was late when the two brothers left the nursing home. "Frank," his brother said, "she's cheating on me again." His brother's marriage was worse than his own. His brother said, "Please, Frank, check for me."

And that was how Frank ended up in the tree. He watched for a full minute, between the red-brown leaves, his sister-in-law with another man. She wore a cowboy hat, and for some reason, Frank found that the most sickening part of the scene. She couldn't take even the cheating seriously. His brother deserved that, at least, that it be done respectfully. He was just about to climb down and tell his brother that nothing was wrong. But then she saw him. She yelled. Frank fell out of the tree, and the two, partially clothed, tumbled out of the house after him. Or that is what his brother told him happened. For a while, Frank couldn't remember anything. For a while, Frank called Hazel by her sister's name, Liz. "Liz is off in college," Hazel said. "Remember?" He didn't.

Ginny tells the priest that novenas aren't going to save anyone.

"Actually," Father Beschler says, "with Vatican II. . . ." Sometimes he says things, though he knows he shouldn't, just to make her angry. She is beautiful when she is angry. Usually, she is pretty. So pretty that he can't look at her without wondering whether he should have been Methodist. Or whatever it is that Ginny is. He would do whatever her religious tracts say. She could have been his beautiful, furious, aged wife. They could have been missionaries, barefoot on some exotic soil, eating yams and berries out of their hands. Does she know that one more word from her could very well sweep him away?

And so, he turns and leaves her, right in the middle of—

"Three hundred left to go!" Frank shouts, and they all turn and cheer. The children throw candy wrappers and ticket stubs in the air. They hardly know why. They just know this feels like New Year's Eve. But they've never stayed up late enough to know what actually happens at midnight.

Jack has bought Hazel and himself turkey dinners. Next year, he will be in high school. Soon, he will have a driver's license. No more turkey dinners after that. From then on, it's nothing but the best for Hazel. The lunch rush is over, and the cafeteria is nearly empty. A few people eat pie. Some stragglers linger over coffee. Tillie and Theresa sit side by side at a table near the wall. Hazel drizzles gravy over everything except the creamed corn. She butters that, and throws a slice of cheese on top. She had asked Alberta for the cheese. Hazel said she couldn't stand to eat corn without it. Jack thinks this will have to change before she comes to have dinner at his house. Dinner is, he knows, the next step. Also, she will have to sit better. She can't sit at his dinner table with one leg bent and up on the chair, like she is now, leaning back and picking apart a bun, rolling it into balls and popping them in her mouth. "You're going to choke," he says. But he doesn't mind. Her neck is beautiful when she throws her head back to catch the bread.

Hazel is amazed and disappointed at the progress her father has made. Two weeks ago, when he couldn't remember anything, Hazel thought she could remedy all of their dysfunctions. Mark has long been out of the house. Liz left for college this year. It is all, simultaneously, more simple and more complex.

She baked her father sweet things: chocolate chip cookies, oatmeal squares, her first pie—blueberry. She brought them on plates that stacked up on the nightstand in Mark's old room, the room Ginny and Hazel had lugged him to when he first came home from the hospital.

Hazel started small. Her father had a bump the size of a foot's heel on his forehead. She invented pets they'd never had—a long-eared bunny, a cow that won grand champion at the state fair, a beagle that howled on command just because she'd always wanted one.

A few days in, she started bringing the family albums and changing the stories around. All of their birthday parties turned out more pleasantly than they actually had. Liz had not thrown the car into the ditch last year and left Frank to tow it out with the tractor. Grandma had not gotten sick. She was out riding horses and would probably stop by to see him soon. Ginny was at work. She'd gotten that job she always wanted and had to work long days. "She visits at night," Hazel said, "while you're asleep."

No one is watching Tillie and Theresa anymore. At first, Tillie was relieved. But now she is suspicious. She watches the gym from where she sits, and everyone is having fun. The children are dancing. They are running. Should Theresa do this, too? Theresa ignores the whole festival and looks at the computer printout over the milk cooler. Their lunch prayer is on it, and she is mouthing the words over and over again. She looks like a dimwit. Tillie bends over, reaches under the table, and pulls two crumpled dollar bills from her purse. "Here," Tillie says, "take these and go play a game."

"That's all right," Theresa says.

"It's all yours—go!"

Theresa has finally become invisible. She says, "I don't really want to."

"Two hundred left to go!" Frank shouts.

Everyone turns, cheers. No one sees Tillie slap Theresa except for Hazel and Alberta. Theresa is good at acting like nothing happened. Her cheek is bright red. She stares straight ahead and mouths the words to herself one more time. Then she slides the money off the table. She heads toward the hallway. She thinks she will go to the ladies' room, close the stall door, and, if no one is in there, cry.

Alberta watches Tillie sit and smile, with her purse on her lap. She remembers the pies. She put them in over two hours ago. When she opens the oven door, smoke billows out. She pulls the pies out with a hot pad and closes the door, fast, before the smoke alarm goes off. But, really, she doubts the alarm works. These things are just for show, for peace of mind.

The pies are hissing. All the old ladies who have been working in the kitchen are gathered around them. They are in awe. Never has any one of them ruined a pie so badly.

The lattice crusts are black and have pulled away from the pie tins. The fruit is shrunken, and between it and the crust is a vast gap, like a jack-o-lantern's mouth.

One of them finally dares to speak. "Well," she says, "out to the pig." *Yes,* they all murmur, *out to the pig.* And so, Alberta takes a pie in each hand and leaves the kitchen, the cafeteria, and goes out the gym door. The beer tent is packed. People linger outside the canvas flap door, smoking cigarettes. For some reason, Alberta feels the need to look away. Not that it's improper for her to be looking at them or that they shouldn't be there, but because it will make them feel uncomfortable, watching her work so hard in the kitchen, struggling, and having to throw whole pies away from the effort. They are young, some of them, and they should feel young without her old eyes on them.

When she gets to the pig's makeshift rig, she waits for a minute and allows herself to lean, just so slightly, on the wire fence. She doesn't want the pig to burn its snout. Then the priest would have to kiss a burned snout on top of everything else. The pig is pinkish-white and ringed thickly with a brown stripe. It is an ugly pig with a hairy face. Frank must have picked the worst one. He must have some beef with the priest. The wind picks up and Alberta shakes off a chill. She nestles the pie tins down into a tuft of straw. "Eat up, little piggie," she says. "Eat up."

The priest is back in the hallway, pacing. He is trying hard to trust himself again, to align his urges with the Greater Urges. The harvest decorations have started to wilt. Bunches of cornstalks gathered at the entranceway are dropping their leaves. They toss around in the breeze coming from under the front door and it feels very much, he thinks, like the Wild West. Some ears of corn have been battered about, a child's sword fight maybe, and kernels litter the floor. Theresa comes out from the bathroom. Her face is blotched with red. She stops to drink at the water fountain and has to snort back the snot before she takes a drink. He should go over there and comfort her, take her in his arms and ask her, finally, if she wants to leave. No, he should tell her it is time for her to go away. But she turns and walks back down the hall, and so the priest, too, turns back and walks the other way.

Then there is a rustling and a shrieking like he has never before heard—the scarecrow must have her—and the priest ducks into the cakewalk. The cakewalk is in the fourth-grade classroom. Desks are pressed to the walls. Bulletin boards are decorated with state capitals and state birds. There is music playing—lullabies. Five children circle around thirty or so pieces of numbered construction paper. The table along the wall is still filled with cakes that must be given away. He gives Mrs. Jones's sister, who is running the record player, a twenty, and says he will play until it runs out. Just tell him when.

When Hazel hears Theresa screaming, she bolts from the cafeteria. Hazel sometimes stares at Theresa kicking gravel, walking the parking lot during lunch recess and thinks *There's someone who has it worse.* But Hazel has never known why, really, Theresa has it worse.

Jack warms his wrists up for the putt-putt competition. His golf instructor says he needs to work on his follow-through.

Ginny eats another piece of pecan pie. She funnels her energy into eating. Talking to the priest is worse than talking to her husband. You can't get anywhere with these men. They think they know everything.

When Hazel realized she could tell her father anything and he would believe it, she told him to shave his beard. She said Ginny liked a smooth face.

Then, she sat on the bed and held her father's hand. She took a deep breath. She realized this would be very different from her romance novels. If she wanted her parents to fall deeply in love, she would have to bring in God. Harlequins never did that.

"Remember being converted?" she asks. "Remember that?" She didn't wait for an answer. She said, "I'll tell you, because I think Ginny is worried you've forgotten. She's worried she's going to come in here and that you'll be some heathen. That's the real reason she hasn't visited." And then Hazel delivered a scene. In the scene, the band played. There was a tuba solo. There were shouts of joy and crying. Her mother held her father tightly and rocked him back and forth. She was so happy. Hazel surprised herself with how well she delivered it all. Once done, she fully expected her father to shout out, *I'm saved!* as soon as Ginny opened the bedroom door. Then, Ginny would believe something miraculous had happened here, in this bedroom. It wouldn't be a miracle, but it would be the next best thing.

But when Ginny opened the door, she just stood there, looking disappointed. She had been waiting for an apology for over a week, and she wasn't afraid to tell Frank exactly what he had to be sorry for.

From his booth, Frank shouts, "Fifty dollars!"

Jack walks aimlessly through the gym with the golf clubs slung across his back like a quiver full of arrows. He is dark and handsome and looks like a young hero stomping the forest, looking for his lady, or something to hunt.

The pig has eaten the insides of both the pies and its belly is burning. Its mouth is frothing. It grunts and grunts until someone pours a beer for it, dividing the liquid between the two pie tins. The pig snorts it up.

Tillie goes up to Alberta and asks her when she might be ready to leave. "I've been ready for some time now," Tillie says.

"Of course," Alberta says. "Anytime." She asks where Theresa is. Tillie feels she has fallen into a trap. She's forgotten Theresa. She thinks as quickly as she can. She says, "Theresa already got a ride home with some friends." But she realizes that would mean Theresa is at home, now, and alone. That looks bad. So, Tillie corrects herself and says, "I mean, she's staying at their house overnight. Very good parents, respectable." Then Tillie realizes that, if she follows through with this, she will be abandoning Theresa at school, and someone will find her, eventually, maybe the janitor, and have to drive her home. They would take her away. It's useless now, the whole act. Tillie sits down at a table and cries behind her purse. Alberta hands her a crumpled napkin.

"We've made it!" Frank shouts. "We've made it!" He is surprised at his own enthusiasm. It's genuine. He jogs, bucket in hand, past Ginny, who is exhausted now and sitting at the pie table, past the putt-putt, past the Yum-Yum tree, and outside, to prep the pig. Behind him, the gym seems to echo, *Get the priest. Find the priest.* Father can hear it from the cakewalk, but he just keeps walking, around and around. He lets the music lull the call away for as long as it can.

The pig is dead. Frank jostles its belly to make sure. He rolls it onto its back. Straw is stuck to its side. He walks back into the gym. No one notices. There is too much bustling and hubbub. He stands in front of Ginny and says, "The pig is dead. What should we do?"

"Make something up," she says. She shrugs. Her shoulders are still beautiful.

Hazel has whisked Theresa away, outside the school. It is windy. The grass is stiff and leaves roll themselves across it. The girls are both shivering and looking through the fence at the pig Hazel's father has just rolled over. They've never seen anything so dead before. Theresa points at the half-eaten pies in the cage.

"Those are Tillie's," she says.

"You sure?" Hazel asks.

Theresa gives her a long look. Her eyelashes are stick-straight and still wet.

No one from the beer tent notices the two girls undo the catch on the fence. There is too much shouting, too much music to hear the rattling and the creaking. Hazel grabs the pig's hind legs. Theresa, the fore. Its hooves are packed with manure and straw. The girls grab its hocks. This is not what Hazel had in mind. No one could find this comforting, except the priest. The pig's tongue is sticking out, and it licks Theresa's leg with each step until Theresa learns to take shorter steps. Theresa keeps her head down and turned to the side. Hazel backpedals. She leads the way to the cornfield behind the school. It is only a few more yards. Hazel tells Theresa that everything will be fine. More than fine. Theresa loses her grip and the pig drops in front of her. Something comes from its mouth with the impact. Theresa shakes her hands and breathes and breathes. "Come on," Hazel says. They get to the edge of the cornfield and weave between the rows, looking for the right spot. Hazel tells Theresa that she will grow up, and that her chin, her lips, will be the most admired in the town. Everyone will want to kiss them. But she will only kiss one with her quivering mouth: a handsome young man, a rescuer. He will hunt the woods and bring her nice things to eat. He will work very hard to deserve her and go through many trials. He will be so nice, so very nice to her.

Fennimore

Harvey had a reputation for being lazy. He was also skilled at odd jobs, indispensable in his own way. From the bedroom window, Marigold watched as he lathered his Bronco and vacuumed sunflower seeds from between the seats. She rolled his boxer briefs and tucked them into his duffel. His white hair was long and oiled. It was heartwarming to see him break a sweat, to see the hair glisten in its ponytail. His only friend in the world was getting married, and they planned to carry out their bachelor exploits in Harvey's Bronco. They'd start the next morning, Wisconsin to San Diego, then up and down the coast. Marigold needed all of that time to think about leaving him.

Harvey worked into the moonlit hours. When Marigold finished his packing, she sat on the porch steps with a glass of jug wine. She tried always to give him space. She did not know how she felt about him. His actions assumed they would live their lives together: meals, church festivals, trips to the grocery—but he was not curious about her. Harvey and Marigold were in their sixties. They were not a couple, and they did not date. She interpreted his behavior toward her this way: That she existed only when his attention was turned toward her. That she entered a dark box when she left his sight. That she was a dog he forgot to pet.

The two lived in an old ceramic brick house that Marigold rented from a farmer. All day, beef cattle grazed the hills. The hay grew beside her. Morning and night, the farmer would walk from his house an acre away and take the gravel path that ran in front of the brick house to the barn, where he heaped scoops of grain and alfalfa into troughs. Some mornings, she followed the farmer at his chores and watched the cows' eager licking into the wooden corners, the wet paths their tongues left, all while she leaned on the fence and drank her morning coffee in her pajamas and bathrobe. The farmer was a widower and couldn't have minded the company.

The farmer could not be a man who said, "It's happening," and then made for the bathroom each morning, as Harvey did. Harvey said the same thing when Marigold bent over to put a pan away or open the oven. He would grab her by the hips so she could feel him harden against her—*It's happening.*

It rarely happened, and even when it did, it was not something they discussed. It was nothing more than a flurry of agitation that melted as soon as it fell over them. Sex was not a reason or a way to think of Harvey. Their relationship was like a body under stress: the attention went directly to the threats, and there was little energy left to tend the unnecessary systems. Harvey suspected the farmer, the tradesmen he dealt with, of shortchanging him, of slights. Harvey often told her how bad their lives were, how unfair and meaningless, and she exhausted herself trying to derail these thoughts before they steamed down the track and ruined their night. The difference of a dollar could cause a day to collapse.

When Harvey finished waxing the truck, he rested his canvas gloves on his knee and looked back at the Bronco. "It looks handsome in this light, doesn't it?" he said. It did. Pearly gray with a fresh red racing stripe. He thought they should go in, have a little sweet, and call it a night. Marigold tilted her head back and failed once more to soak in the multiplying and ceaseless stars. Harvey turned to go inside. He held the door for her and waited.

*

After Harvey left, Marigold sat on the porch swing in her bathrobe, smoking. She drank a deep cup of coffee. The sun was not close to rising and everything was blue. A raccoon waddled up the steps, and she startled it with the swing's creaking. Deer leapt across the fencerow. The hills in front of her stacked one on top of the other and were cut across by a zagging road, rows of pine. When she was young, there were puzzles she would put together with her father where the artist had painted country stores and cider mills, wooden carts heaped with apples. In the flattening pre-dawn dark, she could just as well be another thing the artist drew. The figure on the porch, the old woman.

There was a little house in Fennimore that could be bought for only back taxes. It had been advertised in the shopping news for the past three weeks. The agent told her the house had been abandoned two years ago. It was in a little wood and had a dirt floor and broken windowpanes that, from the look of the paper's photos, birds had used for nesting. The government wanted only what it was owed. Which, the agent had said, was really a song.

Marigold was going to see the house at ten. She would work on her ornaments until nine. But until the farmer came over on the path and she wished him a good morning, she would smoke—a pastime she would not allow herself when Harvey was around. This rule kept her, she believed, from becoming needy. When the itch arose, she imagined putting a hand on his soft-haired chest and with only the slightest push, sending him back into another room as if he were a pillar of hot air.

Headlights shone across Marigold's porch, and a black Escort pulled into the farmer's driveway. The car's music quieted on the garage pad. It was the farmer's daughter, and she was wearing her green canvas jacket and bedroom slippers. She slammed the car door, then dropped her keys while trying to unlock the trunk. T-shirts on wire hangers slid one on top of the other in her clothesbasket, and one hooked into the basket's weave, dangling. She tripped while walking to the front door and caught herself on the garage. The floodlights switched on, and the farmer stood by the door in his flannel shirt with both hands on the small of his back. His body was still waking. She dropped the clothesbasket on the cement and began to cry.

Marigold had only seen the daughter from afar, during the rare but extended periods the woman spent with her father. The daughter had been studying to be an artist for years now. "She must have a doctorate in art," Marigold once said to the farmer, as a joke. "That seems to be the idea," the farmer had said. He'd had an aunt who had been a silent film star in Hollywood. He believed his daughter must have caught something from her, some recessed gene. Marigold could not understand how such a practical man could encourage this kind of daughter, that lifestyle, the looseness and impractical anger. She assumed the woman used the place as a hideout, a stop between bad lovers. Marigold did not doubt the daughter's green jacket had once been the farmer's. Marigold could imagine its scent—straw and Lava hand soap.

*

The house in Fennimore had no ceiling, but rafters under the steel roof where the previous tenant had stored wooden warehouse boxes on top of the beams. The agent was a large woman with a short perm who had once worked repair on Maytag appliances. She pointed toward the boxes with a yellow broom and told Marigold that whatever was in the boxes would go along with the house. No one was about to go looking in them and stirring up trouble.

There was a brick fireplace on one end of the open room. Broken-off mortar cascaded down its angled chimney, a metal grate held back ash and logs and bits of aluminum can. Marigold contemplated owning the fireplace and depending on it for heat. She tapped the grate with her foot. A log rolled over to reveal a length of singed squirrel. She turned and looked down the long space. There was no basement, of course, but she had not considered what was meant by a dirt floor. There was ceramic tile in the kitchen, and its grouting had been broken apart by the dirt settling unevenly, and by the gulches that ran underneath a sodden layer of phone books. If looked at from a distance, which was how Marigold was looking, the tiles rose up like steps to the refrigerator, which looked new and was propped on cinderblocks. The stove was on blocks, too. There was hard-plank flooring throughout the rest of the house, and this had grayed and splintered as baseball bleachers do, with hardened splotches of orange and green fungus. The sharpness had gone out of the wood's creak. Sickly yellow quack grass grew along the wide gaps. The plaster walls were blue and faded. They hung like stiff draperies near the floor.

"Has this place been tested for mold?" Marigold asked.

"No," the agent said. "Let's be clear—" The woman caught her breath and watched a toad panting in the corner. "This house is a rogue stallion. It does what it wants."

The bedroom was a paneled-off area near the fireplace. Marigold opened the plywood door. It was a dark, pathetic room with a wide window too high up to look out. She imagined falling asleep on a mildewed mattress while wearing a little white mask over her mouth and nose. And then, eventually, she would not wake up. That was how her life would end.

"It was a sportsman's shack," the agent said. "Man came and went. Probably trampled by a deer like that hunter up in Beaver Dam."

When the agent remembered her job, she said, "The right handyman could fix this up."

Marigold broke into wild laughter—a burst that left her breathless with the excess cackling. She imagined Harvey doing such a thing, leaving his work varnishing the kitchen table to shoo a toad out the door, herding it with his handkerchief. It was a joke. The house would be another period of long work for her, an extended loneliness.

Later that afternoon, the first that Harvey was gone, Marigold sat on the porch swing and watched the traffic go by. Homecoming week must have kicked off at the high school. Junkers were tearing down the tractor road with toilet paper flying from the windows and signs that read *Master and Mistress* and other nonsense. The high schoolers hollered and screamed over the road's humps and potholes. They were drunk, and circling through the backroads on a loop to avoid the sheriff, a purgatory of flirtation by fear. When Marigold was about to go in, the farmer's daughter came out and sat on his bench. She painted her toenails. It didn't take long for the woman to tread, toes erect, toward the road. When the next truck came over the hill, she took aim and gunned the polish into the open window of the extended cab. Red polish looped through the air and landed with the splatter of sudden rainfall on the truck. The driver squealed rubber onto the sealcoat in his getaway.

When the daughter turned, she saw Marigold. She walked, still careful, along the gravel road, until she reached the edge of Marigold's lawn.

"I was once the homecoming queen," she said. "I have certain unalienable rights."

Before Marigold could respond, the farmer came out with his good flannel on, holding his daughter's bedroom slippers. He waved at Marigold, and the daughter made her way back over the rise. The two went in his station wagon toward town, probably to get fried cod and cheese from the gas station. Marigold wondered whether he knew the types of things artists did.

*

There were reasons for Marigold and Harvey to live together. Marigold had lost money in her divorce, the recession had hit her nest egg, her father had died a debtor, and her childhood home had been auctioned. After her father's death, acquaintances had encouraged her to move out east, near them, to take in the culture. She easily could have found work as an accountant. Marigold thought of all the times she had bought plane tickets and booked hotels in New York or DC to see art, ballet, the heavy wines and the steaks she'd eaten with her ex, and felt sick. That was her old life. It was dead to her.

Harvey mowed the church lawn. One day, Marigold had waved to him while bringing daffodils to her father's grave. She'd waved as a courtesy. It wasn't until he stopped the mower that she recognized him. There had been a history, a romance—no, only a high school dance, preceded by weeks in Chemistry when Harvey untied the strings of her rubber lab apron each time he walked by. A flirtation that neither mentioned.

Marigold kept her workspace in the second living room. She made Christmas ornaments and sold them online for eighty dollars apiece. They were made from antique silk and gold-dipped beading and freshly lacquered cutouts from old greeting cards. Two feet of ribbon trailed down the tree from each hook—her signature. It was therapy, from all of those years spent working with numbers. On her desk, pliers and fishing line. A neat row of adhesives. In drawers, the endless layers of stuff scoured from the garage sale circuit each summer, the church basements and thrift stores in the winter. Behind her desk, near a window, she kept a Christmas tree, and would photograph each ornament as she finished it. Her eternal season of hope.

She gave the farmer an ornament each Christmas. He gave Marigold and Harvey several white paper packs of beef patties. Harvey went wild for them, baked in a pan with barbecue sauce.

*

Harvey sent a photo of the beach. Later, a short video of himself at the wheel of the Bronco while "All the Old Cowboys" played on the radio. He bought a pair of expensive jeans two sizes too small.

Marigold took it in. She grew to resent that he did not ask after her or her decision of whether to move out, though she knew full well he hadn't the slightest. Her thoughts began to fester, and she took to marching around the farmer's fields, scaring the cattle by kicking the cracked cornstalks and wearing Harvey's old coonskin getup.

*

The second week that Harvey was gone, Marigold didn't bother stopping by the post office, or the gas station for a cup of coffee. She didn't approach her ornaments, either. The Christmas tree stood in the good lighting all day, naked, save five unsold pieces and the garland. At night, she would plug in the twinkling lights and let herself be absorbed into some kind of jaded humor. She tossed things around and listened to them clatter. She wore soft cloth shorts with wide pockets and reclined on the couch, smoking—something she never allowed herself to do in the house. She'd stopped wishing the farmer a good morning. His schedule had been off since the daughter's return, and Marigold felt like the least important woman in the world and marveled that she was still alive. She would look around while on the couch and calculate how many resources it took just to keep her in this lowly state—fed, rented, and pathetically clothed. It was criminal. She should be sent to Siberia.

One night, she put on lipstick, then turned on all the lights in the house. She began to flip her bedroom light switch on and off frantically. These hills played tricks with the eye. There was a wild hope someone would believe the house was on fire. Many times, a lit house received a second look, a call from a neighbor a bend or two away. Marigold wanted the call. She flipped the switch. The bed, where she'd thrown a dusky negligée, her flat, unpainted toes, the bedside table strewn with snotted tissues became one illuminated afterimage that glowed when her eyes were closed. She stopped only when she had to catch herself on the doorframe from dizziness.

Marigold spent Wednesday morning getting up from the table and pulling the curtain back to look at the grass accumulating in lush clumps. She wondered if the lawn needed cutting. In the afternoon, she realized she could no longer avoid it. It had been the same story with leg hair when she was young. Marigold looked down at her thin legs, the broken veins, the wrinkles circling the knee. She was wasting the day in the same way she'd wasted her youth.

She let the ditches have it and was sorry she'd postponed the pleasure so long. It was wonderful, to yank the push mower up and down the inclines and send the stray gravel flying out the chute, out toward the feral, whorish barn cats.

Harvey had won a little jackpot in a casino and sent a photo of himself fanning the bills and wearing a camouflage cap while he stood next to the slot machine. He could not fit the cash in his wallet, and wrote that while he walked along the beach, the money would erupt from his tight back pocket and fly into the Pacific wind. It was all he and his friend could do to keep the money out of the ocean. They decided to spend some of the winnings at a strip club. Harvey told Marigold how he could not get a lap dance—each time the dancer spread his legs to dance between them, his new jeans slowly pulled his legs back together. Eventually the three sat down for a beer and a chat in the private space they'd rented. The dancer had an octopus tattooed over her most intimate parts, and his friend had not been able to get over it—over the artistry, Harvey said. Some very intricate work had been done.

Some chat, Marigold thought. While Marigold mowed, she imagined octopus legs flying through the air, the suction cups quivering for a hold. The beak, grounded. She would not compete with the memory of a stripper, she told herself. Not at her age.

*

Thursday morning, Marigold called the agent and made plans to see the house again the next day. She had eaten a full supper and a breakfast of scrambled eggs with a slice of cold pie. She finished three ornaments, and in the afternoon, she stopped by the gas station for a soft serve cone that she ate at the river park, strolling and making small talk with the campers. There were rumors of thunderstorms coming that night, and travelers were pulling their potted impatiens and folding chairs into the RVs. The children ran around in a group with baseball bats pointed at the sky and taunted their parents by calling for lightning to strike.

The next day, the power was out. The sky was dark, the rain had stopped, and it was only the thundering that woke Marigold in time to get to Fennimore. She went without coffee and used a flashlight to see where to put her eyeliner. Out in the garage, with the car running, she pressed the garage door opener. She pressed it five times before she realized it would not open.

When she walked across the lawn to the farmer's house, it was with the idea that he would help her hoist the door. It was nine o'clock. Before she got to the front door, Marigold saw the farmer's daughter, who was walking through the wet grass toward her. She had a steak in one hand that she held by width of the T, and was chewing. Marigold could not help but think, as the daughter walked toward her and she saw her up-close for the first time, that the daughter behaved as though she were prettier than she was, and younger.

Marigold shaded her eyes, though it was dark, and called out to ask how she was.

The daughter kept walking, and Marigold wasn't sure the daughter had heard until the woman was within reach. "I'm dying," she said.

"Oh."

"No, I'm just—" The daughter interrupted herself and looked down at the steak in her hands. There was patience in this long look, for herself and the meat. "I think I'm just a little low on iron. Do you know what I mean?" She looked imploringly at Marigold, as though she needed to be understood on a level deeper than minerals.

Marigold said she did.

"I feel like I can't see. I mean, it's like I don't have eyes until I eat something meaningful."

Marigold stared at the daughter until she replied, "Your dad says something like that."

"We're peasant stock. Still recovering from the hunger. Something genetic."

There was a rumbling in the valley, and a hawk landed on the farmer's TV antenna. The daughter's jacket flapped as the wind picked up and she considered which bite to take next. Marigold watched. She was trying to understand whether or not this woman was smart.

"Is there something I can help you with?" the daughter asked. "My father's up at the gas station getting coffee. The electric's out and we need a paper. Who knows what's happened while we slept."

*

The daughter's car smelled like the '90s. Cigarette smoke and a chemical dampness, as though a cleaning had gone wrong. Marigold cranked the passenger window up as they approached the highway and the rain began again. The daughter's name was Sonia.

"I have only AM radio or Meat Loaf. The tape was stuck in the deck when I bought the car. I don't mind it anymore."

The two listened to AM radio until the National Weather Service siren interrupted and a long line of flood warnings followed. Lightning struck a mailbox. They drove on, and the daughter switched the wipers to full. A fire truck was parked at the feed implement, to keep watch for tornados. Sonia slowed and set the headlights at high-beam and sighed a wretched, throaty sigh. Marigold thought the woman might cry. Instead, she pushed play on the tape deck.

"Meat Loaf is so sad," Sonia said. "He never learns what love is."

Once they reached downtown Fennimore, Marigold directed the daughter off the highway and past the school and the dairy until they arrived at the house. They parked beside a row of pine trees. By then, the rain had calmed to a drizzle. Sonia stopped the engine.

The two sat looking at the place and its aluminum siding until the agent called Marigold's cell phone and said she was stuck on one side of a flooded ravine. She told Marigold where a spare key was kept hidden and stayed with her on the line until she'd found it in the grassy center of a deflated tire down the hill.

Inside the house, Sonia stood over a shallow reflecting pool that had gathered between the kitchen and living room. Marigold asked whether she had rubber soles. She wanted to try out the lighting and didn't want to—

"Fry me?"

"It's not as bad as I remember," Marigold lied. "These cabinets," she opened two beside the refrigerator, "could hold a lot of plates. Or books. Isn't that what they do in the city? Keep their shoes in the oven?"

"I used to keep my students' still lifes in the dishwasher. Lots of pitchers and bowls of eggs and rotting eggplant."

Marigold watched as Sonia batted away a mosquito and turned toward the bathroom. "Does this toilet work?"

"I don't know," Marigold said. "I'd look in it before I did anything."

While the daughter was gone, Marigold stood in the center of the space. She felt a breeze coming in and listened to the birds shake off the storm with chirping. Moving was all she could think to do to set Harvey straight where he didn't understand he was crooked.

Sonia returned quietly. She kept her mouth shut and took her time looking into Marigold's eyes, studying her face. The way a lover gazes his way into the beloved's feelings. Marigold felt an unfolding relief, to be looked at that way.

"I won't tell you what I saw in there," Sonia said. She looked away, up, into the rafters.

"What's that?"

"In the bathroom. If you want to know, you'll have to go in there yourself."

Marigold took the yellow-handled broom from the corner and tried to brush the pools of water out toward the door. She wasn't ready to tell Sonia that she wanted to go and to never return. Sonia kept looking up.

"Do you know what's in those boxes?" she asked.

There were two tall chairs set up near the kitchen island, and the women stood on them and finagled one of the warehouse boxes between the rafters and let it drop to the floor. The crate was four by five feet, and about as tall. When it fell, the floorboards shook, and the lid opened and belched a cloud of dust before it fell back into place.

"We'll say it was vandals," Sonia said, and stepped down from the chair. She wiped spiderwebs from her hands onto the front of her jacket, and they hung in the air as she moved. "High schoolers. Undergraduates."

The box was made of wood and had two-by-fours running diagonally along the sides. It came up to Marigold's shoulders, and she could imagine the peace she would find if she were to climb into it and lock herself in with its iron clasp. "This box would be big enough, wouldn't it?" she asked. "I could live in here." Marigold wanted no one to take seriously the thing she said, including herself.

She bent to open the box, but Sonia stopped her by leaning squarely on the lid.

"You will die if you live here. That's why the owners left, because they were dead."

"I've got thirty years on you."

"They had to be removed. They did not die from peaceful old age."

Sonia made a noise like a mule, or some other beast of burden, before she threw the lid off the crate.

Inside, the head of a black bear cub was swaddled in pelts of soft brown and auburn and calico. Ram's horns stood along the right side, twisting through mounds of fur and leather. An alligator's spine rolled along the side nearest Sonia, and Marigold grew dizzy, following the notches as they seemed to round the corner and move toward her. Moths flew out, and it took Marigold a full minute to see the small white larvae moving along the cub's balding head before she stumbled back and fell on a loose kitchen tile.

The daughter leaned over with her hands behind her back to look more closely at the pile. A moth walked along her collarbone. Marigold wondered how often this woman's heart had been wrung dry just as badly as her own.

*

They took only what would fit in the one box and tied Sonia's trunk closed over it with twine. Sonia flushed the agent's spare key down the toilet and insisted they hurry. "Some things were never meant to be in use," she said. That night, the two women placed the furs in black contractor's bags and sprayed them with Raid, then let them set that way until the day Harvey was scheduled to return.

They shampooed the pelts that morning. Marigold hung a dark red bull's hide out to dry on the porch railing. The long tail dripped into the bushes.

"You'll scare people straight with this production," the farmer told them on his way back from chores. They had been kneeling on the porch planks, massaging suds into a fox's fur. "They'll think you keep a shotgun behind the door like those wild people in Texas. Like those cowboys."

"That's the idea," Sonia had said, and kept scrubbing. "Scare away the yahoos. Tell the weaklings to git." She was a good daughter. When she blasted the pelts with the garden hose, clumps of fur came loose. The evergreen shrubs along the porch looked as though they had contracted mange. The barn swallows dove to gather it for nests and Sonia waved them away with a wet towel.

The wolf and coyote hides still held the top of the heads, and had been fitted with glass eyes that rolled loosely about the sockets. The leg leather from three tanned alligator bellies flapped to the sides, against the railing spokes, in the gentle fall breeze. There were deerskins and moose rack. Strings of teeth and claws. The black noses had an ocher mold bubbling on them that Marigold had rubbed clean with alcohol. The stuffed bear cub was posed on his hind legs and reached up his arm as if he held a lantern, or a dagger. Marigold placed him at the bottom of the porch steps.

After they finished, Sonia sat on the porch swing and let the soapy foam dry on her hands. She wore cut-off shorts and her legs were wet and downy. "If you can spare that coyote, I think I have a use for it," she said.

*

Marigold brought out coffee mugs and poured jug wine, and the two women sat on the porch, drinking, until the sun went down and the fireflies were no longer interesting.

"I'm liable to miss supper at this rate," Sonia said. She stretched and let herself fall against a porch pillar.

"Hold on," Marigold said. "I think we have something a little better in here." She held onto the stairs, and then pushed herself slowly up them. Inside, on the lazy Susan, she found a nearly empty bottle she saved for toddies. It was covered with a sticky dust and the top was stuck. The kitchen light was harsh and fluorescent on the ivies by the window, and she watched as they seemed to wind across the open shelves, which were speckled with toast crumbs. None of her dishes matched, and Harvey kept his spare, oil-spattered tools in a gallon ice cream bucket by the refrigerator. The amber ends of plastic bread bags stuck out from the drawers beside the sink, and Marigold was surprised by them. The kitchen was alien to her. She turned off the light and waited. Her heart was racing from too much wine.

Marigold turned to go outside. Through the screen door, she could see Sonia surrounded by furs, listening to the cattle lowing in the pasture. In the dark, the furs were black mounds rounded over the porch railing and glistening in the scant light. Beside the screen door were broad windows and that tree with its plastic boughs. Marigold lit the twinkling strands, and the bulbs shone across the red lacquer of her ornaments, the gold finish and the empty pearls.

The ribbon ends trailed down. It was approaching midnight, and Harvey hadn't returned.

Outside, a bear kept watch over the steps in the darkness. But who could see it well enough to be afraid? A hunter can stalk his prey for days and wind up with nothing more than some leather, rolled tight and slid under a bed, or something that feels as hollow as a woman whose hope has flown out the window. What living thing could have been in that box to fuel a soul through winter?

Passing

I.

There is a blackjack in the house. It's thin and rounded like a pear, and the leather is softened from its day-to-day beatings. There are four thick exposed seams and, within the seams, several lead pellets. When shaken, it sounds like a toy, or a maraca. At its narrow end is a rawhide strap, large enough for a hand to slip through, for it to dangle from the wrist—the hand in the pocket, looking nonchalant. It once belonged to one Marcus Pertle, a member of the Chicago police force who was retired, with honors, in 1890. The blackjack was Pertle's weapon of choice. He never left a mark.

Frank takes the blackjack from the drawer and displays it in his palm, flipping it once to show off its wholeness and simplicity. Much like a carpenter displays a chair that has been carved from a single log. Frank feels satisfied, not only with the blackjack but with the day, which is sunny. There is a roast in the oven for a big fall lunch. Hazel is home. Jack is with her. They live four hours away, in Iowa. But it might as well be Texas. They hardly visit.

"Ever seen one of these?" he asks Jack. Frank takes the blackjack and slaps it into the fatty part of his hand. Too hard. Frank has to turn and shake his hand out. The luxury of showing weakness—this is new to Frank, particularly around Jack. Frank wishes it were new to Jack. But Jack has taken a step back and is shaking his head dumbly, as if to prove he is stuck on being delicate. Frank had spent over ten years trying to menace him away from his daughter, the intensity crescendoing until "Fine," he said, "take her." And now here is Frank, telling his daughter's fiancé what's to be his and where he can find it when Frank conks out. Which might be any day now. When the jig's up, the jig's up. And they hardly visit.

"They're illegal," Frank says.

"But they're not lethal, are they?"

"Oh sure, it could kill you."

*

There is a rocking chair in the house. The wood is solid. The varnish is worn. The seat was once a flat oak sheet. Now it is curved from the skirts wearing it out and greased from the supper hands and the dish hands, hands thick with bacon fat and butter wiped on the back of the skirt. A wooden rosary circles the right arm. The beads lock into one another firmly. The entire chain has, no doubt, been carved from a single piece of wood, bead locking into bead. Ginny has spent hours twirling and twirling the beads around, looking for an end and finding none. The crucifix alone is iron. The chair first belonged to a Catherine Morovitz, who each night would call "Nine bells! Nine bells!" and her children would gather round for Bible and prayers and bed.

The chair fits Ginny just fine. She holds the end of the rosary out to her daughter and says, "Now. You'd have to be careful with this. It's not a toy. The wood gets dry and then one hard yank from a rowdy kid—it's ruined." Hazel nods. Ginny is sure Hazel is not really listening. She is also sure Hazel will not have kids, which is why Hazel gets the chair in the first place. If she does have children, they will probably be languid and inward, and not notice the woodworking. And suddenly Ginny is seized with the question of what is worse: the not noticing or the hard yank? God help her, she doesn't know. And bless Hazel's womb, whatever happens in it. And Jack, of course. He'll need it.

"Here," she says to Hazel. "Try it out."

Hazel sits. The chair is too short for her, and her knees bend too close to her chest. A baby and a pillow would never fit. There would be smothering. "Oh," Hazel says, and moves her arms up and down the chair's arms, as if this will help. Then she splays her legs in front of her. She looks up, and Ginny can't remember the last time her daughter looked up at her like this, with such confusion. "Is this how it's supposed to be?"

"Well," she says, "people were shorter then. And I read in *Prevention* that this kind of angle is good for arthritic knees."

Hazel gives her a look. Ginny says, "None of us is getting any younger."

*

On both Frank's and Jack's hands are boxing gloves. Two pairs. They were once red-dyed goatskin but have faded from being left in a box near the window. The leather is cracked along each of the gloves' bulbous knuckles. When Frank slid them on, his palms grew sweaty. The gloves fit tighter than they used to when he boxed with his brother in their front yard. Before Jack would put his hands into his set, he looked inside each one and shook it out over the grass. "Where'd you say you were storing these?" he asked. "The barn? Many mice there?" Now Jack is dancing in them, moving the gloves through the air like a girl playing a clapping game. Frank is glad they don't have neighbors, that they live in the middle of nowhere. The laces, slapping against his wrists, the leather, sound like a skipping rope.

Frank just stands there. His heels sink into the muddy grass. The gloves hang from his hands like barbells he can't pull up. Jack is the same size his brother was, which is to say, much larger than Frank. When did he grow so muscled? Jack's a book man. These arms are unnatural on him. That's why he can't use them properly. When Frank boxed his brother, Frank would have his sister tie his straps tight, so tight the blood couldn't run to his fingers, and they'd be numb until suppertime, when he would just be able to fumble enough with his fork to get his potatoes down. Looking at his brother standing across from him made his hands sweat so that he was sure the gloves would slip clear off if he even dared to throw a punch. And so, his brother beat him good every time. His father bought the gloves because he thought it'd be a nice show now and then, something to look forward to after the pigs were fed and the cows milked. It never was. His sister said she couldn't watch anymore. "Look at it," she'd said to her father. "Just look at it," she'd say, and the porch door would slam. Frank hated the pity.

Frank walks up to Jack and gives him a solid uppercut just under the ribcage. Jack crumples over. "Come on," Frank says. "There's more stuff over here."

The women stand at the window and watch the men.

"Frank should be more careful with him," Ginny says. Hazel waves the idea off. She is smiling, watching as Jack unfolds himself and limps along, following her father.

Ginny continues rifling through the box. She holds up a barometer painted with flowers and tractors. The arrow points to *very humid.* She looks outside again, at the bedsheets snapping on the clothesline. She hands the barometer to Hazel. "It's broken, I think." Hazel nods and sets it on the pile of collector's pillows and crystal she has accrued in the last half hour. She shows no interest, and Ginny is running out of elaborate backstories to make the items meaningful. Ginny is tempted to just dump the box at Hazel's feet. *Inheritance,* Ginny wants to say. *This is what you get.* What would inspire the necessary reverence, the quiet urgency, that Ginny feels would be appropriate? Ginny picks a cloth-covered book from the box and starts to read it. Might as well. Every few pages there are outlines of shoes and arrows. She flips back to the cover. *Dancing: All the Latest Steps* by Betty Lee. Copyright 1907.

"Now, this—this is interesting," Ginny says, and holds the purple cover up for Hazel to see while she reads aloud: *Dancing should be enjoyed, along with other diversions, in moderation. Increasingly, doctors are prescribing doses of dance to cure melancholia, among other diseases.*

"When was the last time you danced?"

Hazel shrugs. "We used to dance in church sometimes," she says. "Remember?"

Ginny nods. For the past several years, Hazel has been disappearing. Her frame, narrowing. Her quietness grown like a plot of land around her, a plot she's painstakingly cleared and on which she suffers no intruders. Ginny had thought her sad—a thirty-year-old girl, wandering from job to job, staying unemployed for long stretches of time. And what—reading? Watching soap operas? Ginny wonders if her daughter is just dying to the world, like Ginny taught her, and so much more quickly than Ginny ever could. Dying to this world and getting ready for the next. Before she even knows what a husband is, or a child. And if that is the case, then Ginny is jealous. Ginny has attachments: this broken barometer, a silver candy dish. A decorative gong hanging from a wooden stand. It all means so much to her. Ginny takes the gong's small mallet and raps it.

"You were always good in church," Ginny says.

"I bet Jack would like this book," Hazel says, taking it from her mother and handling the pages too roughly. "We'd better hide it."

From outside, there are three quick gunshots. Frank's.

The Remington 700 was purchased for a hunting trip in 1970. Ginny went with Frank, and Frank's brother. They were hunting deer in Sheboygan. Ginny had broken apart from the other two and set up in the bushes. She felt wise, sitting there in her camo. She'd followed tracks, and the other two were drinking and rustling. They would chase the deer right down to her. A doe pranced by and Ginny lowered her rifle to shoot. Then she heard a crack, and a bullet whizzed by her ear so close she could feel its heat. She fell back into the bushes.

"What a shot, Frank," his brother said. "You couldn't hit a barn." Ginny fought something off then, a scream or a shot fired off in their direction, above their heads and into the trees. But what would they have done, apologized? Would Frank do that in front of his brother? Instead, she kept quiet and they marched on past her.

"Why would he give Jack that gun?" Hazel asks.

"Where else would it go? Your brother?"

Hazel shakes her head as if all the world's problems started with her brother, and him not taking this gun is the least of it. She gathers her pile of stuff from the kitchen table and moves it over to a glass-topped stand that's just big enough for a chimney lantern and—if someone or two were sitting on the chairs set next to it—a couple of mugs, two tea plates. A souvenir pincushion from San Francisco slides from the pile to the floor.

"That stand's yours, too."

Hazel takes a deep, patient breath. Ginny has heard more of these from her daughter than she thinks she deserves. "What's the story with the stand?" Hazel asks. From the way her daughter is acting, one more story will break her back. Hazel falls into one of the chairs and rolls her neck. And then what would happen, after her back was broken? Would all her secrets tumble out? Ginny starts. "In 1910, when your great-aunt Sylvia, or maybe it was June, was pregnant and didn't have any idea where—"

The door opens behind them. It's Jack. His stride is fast and all boyishness. He comes around the corner, into the living room. His boots still on and muddy. He's on the carpet and he says, "Look what your dad gave me." He uncups the blackjack from his palm and, in his own grand way, lets it drop onto the stand.

After the crack sounds through the room, Hazel lifts the blackjack, very slowly, with two fingers. The glass is shattered but still holding everything, like it's all caught in a spiderweb. Ginny is glad for the interruption. She couldn't remember the story. But now the stand is gone, gone. Hazel shakes the fat end of the blackjack at him. "Where did you get this?" Hazel asks. "You could kill somebody with this."

Frank stands in the doorway behind them. He calls, "Who left this door open? You're letting all the flies in." Frank closes the door, and now the house is quiet. You can hear the flies buzz. Frank clomps off his boots. Ginny can imagine them, sitting there in the doorway, crisscross on their sides, just waiting to trip her when she goes out for a smoke. Which she will need to, soon.

Hazel stares at Jack. Jack looks past Hazel to the door and says, "Frank—"

The glass buckles under everything Hazel has piled on. When it gives, it sounds like music, all the glass pieces hitting the ornate iron bottom. The chimney lantern, too, gets busted. And all those things—the spoons, the teacups, Betty Lee's book—all go swooshing down through the metal ring. Ginny remembers she bought the table at a garage sale and that she'd talked to the woman who sold it for quite a long time. All of the woman's children had grown and moved down to Florida, so she was selling her things and chasing after them.

II.

In Hazel, there is a baby the size of an avocado. Hazel says she can feel the fingernails, the toenails growing, the baby tearing its way around inside her. The legs are hardening. The eyes are locking into place. So are the ears, and the jagged pattern of bones in the head. Jack loves the baby. It explains everything about Hazel that usually worries him: lapses into silence, terribly long visits to the supermarket, moodiness. Before, he would start to think things, start to worry about her and whoever was with her, because there was probably somebody with her. Some guy—nothing serious, a fling. A series of flings. But now, it's simple. She's pregnant.

They have been exiled, Frank and Jack, from the house. It is almost noon, and there is a roast beef in the oven. It was sad to leave the house once he'd gotten a whiff of it. But Hazel had told him to look at what he'd done, to just look at it, so many times that Ginny took him by the shoulders and led him to the door. "We'll clean this up and then—" She shrugged and walked back to the mess. At lunch, Jack was going to tell everyone the news. But now? Maybe he'll have to put it off again.

Frank says, "I was going to wait to show you this, but—" He walks on, through the garage and out the door. "Well, we've got time." Jack wonders, while they walk down the hill to the shed, who will get the land. There are woods, oats, some cows, the river. There is grass all around. But the road signs along their property are shot out. Beer cans tossed by the mailbox. Tire rubber laid out on the sealcoat. Down a little farther, there is a ditch with an oven in it. He could live on the land, even though they'd once walked the fencerow and found two femurs and, a few yards more, a rib cage. It was an isolated incident, and probably a deer. But beyond their land? He would have to put up an electric fence.

"Ta-da!" Frank says. He produces the largest sled Jack has ever seen, propped up along the wall, but Jack can't focus on that yet. First, he finds the axe that's resting in the corner, the shiny end on the floor and webbed by a long-legged spider and her tawny pouch of eggs. There are round-saw blades running along the wall, rust eating from the outside in from all the wet lumber Ginny had told Frank not to cut. Frank should be a better listener. Jack has thought this as often as Ginny has said it. Empty Folgers cans take up the whole of the table that runs along the wall. In them, screws and nails divided by size and age, syringes and bottles of medicine for the cattle, and chains—linked log chains to hold the dog they used to have, Sandy—and some more intricate weaves that Jack can't place. All these coffee cans remind Jack of Coffee Woods, down the road. There, a farmer killed his wife and chopped her up into pieces he could fit in coffee cans, then planted her throughout the woods. It took years for anyone to figure out. When Frank tells the story, he always ends with one strange laugh. Like he still can't believe it. The strangeness of the laugh reassured Jack during the days when he was sure Frank would knock him out with no hesitation. Resting near the end of the table is a ball of twine cradling a mouse.

Frank is telling a story. "The chickens liked laying eggs, there, under the coop," he said. He spreads his hands a foot or less apart and crouches: that's what it was like to get the eggs out from under the coop—the gap between the building's bottom and the ground was so tight, he had to shimmy to get them because he was the smallest. The swallowed-up feeling. And there were spiders, he was saying, and the chickens would peck at him, and when it rained, there were pools and mud. "But you have to get all the eggs."

One muddy day, when Frank was fourteen and his brother sixteen, his brother said, "Why don't you lie on the sled, and I'll just slide you under?" Frank said, "We could try." So, Frank lay, belly down, on the wooden sled, and his brother slid him under. And left him. The chickens were pecking and the spiders were dropping, crawling, and Frank felt the air running out. The sled railing sloped up in the back and under the coop. It worked like a cage. Frank had to shimmy back down to the farthest end and try to push the sled back in the mud, using just his forearms. It took an age. The eggs were cracked, yolk crushed against his chest.

This is Frank traumatized. He is staring off to the far wall of the shed, where there is a road sign for Broulliard Hill, a once nearby road that no longer exists. Frank knows fear. This is news to Jack, and he is unsure what to do with it. Jack looks up at the sled. It is at least two feet taller than him, and it's propped at an angle. Four or five feet wide. "It sure is a big sled," Jack says.

"It is." Frank turns so that he stands next to Jack, and they look the sled up and down its runners. "I stuck my knife in my brother's tire the next week. A Buick '49, blue fenders. That was a mistake."

*

In the house, the roast beef cannot be avoided. The smell has curled into the corner of every room and worked its way into the fibers of every throw pillow that Hazel has pushed in her face when nobody was looking. She takes slow, measured breaths and sits on the carpet, cross-legged, like a yogi. She has brought out a small rubber tub. Each item is gone over carefully. First it is shaken, then pounded, then picked at with tweezers. When she can run her hands over the pillow without pricks, it can go in the tub.

The glass sounds beautiful when she sifts through it. Like a wind chime. She is half-tempted to run her hands through it, the way a mother might check the temperature for a bath she's drawing. But she is sane, balanced. Ginny is in the kitchen, sticking the meat with a fork and waggling it around, worrying it to perfection. It is burning, Hazel can smell, at the edges.

Ginny comes in the living room. She wipes her hands dry and looks out the window. "They're coming back from the shed," Ginny says. "We better hurry this up." She looks down at Hazel. She had meant Hazel better hurry this up. Hazel knows she has lost whatever sympathy she had earlier in the day. Her mother likes Jack. He is attentive. Her mother is spiritual. When her mother got God, Hazel would fret and shake right next to her in the pews, or in the basement, or wherever they would be. Before then, Hazel always thought she could just as easily be swept out the door with the table crumbs. And she told Jack all of it. He loved to listen. He shook his head in junior high and said, "You are so *exotic.*" He was from the nice street in town. He golfed. He would take hold of her hair, pull her face to his, kiss her forehead. "I don't think you know what that word means," she whispered.

Then something snapped. Probably something important, like a tendon in the leg. She couldn't take the murmuring, the supplications. She didn't want anyone hanging on her words. She would come home from school and her father would say, "Park the car here" or "Throw the hay bales there," and walk away. Directives—why had she never noticed their muscled rhythm before? Jack would ask, "How does that make you feel? The bossing?" He would twirl the ends of her hair like they were flowers and then tuck them behind her ear. Hazel would shrug. Once, while she washed their dishes, Jack walked in, slapped his hand on the countertop, and said, "Now listen here." So powerfully, a hot buzz raced through her. Then he laughed and the buzz passed. He was imitating someone from work. And now, when she isn't frustrated to laziness, she's trying to make him mad. Or tough. Or something more than a pair of pecs. He loves listening. He loves the gym. It helps him feel centered.

Once Hazel has bagged all the big shards of glass, she wrestles the vacuum from the closet. Ginny is still standing by the window, watching everything she does. Shoes tumble from the closet. A jacket falls from its hanger. Hazel kicks the shoes back in.

"I'll get it later," Hazel says, and plugs the vacuum in.

"Your father told me a story this week. About how his brother tricked him and trapped him under the chicken coop for God knows how long."

"Yeah?"

"And when your father got, out he knifed your uncle's tire. It was their only car."

Hazel nods. "That's a good story." She flips the vacuum on. She thinks the roar might drown out Ginny's stare, but no luck there. The vacuum rumbles to a stop.

"Is there a moral I didn't get?"

"Don't leave people in the lurch, Hazel!"

Hazel vacuums and vacuums. Frank and Jack come in. Jack sticks his nose up in the air and tells Ginny the roast smells perfect. She bows, thanks him. Hazel keeps vacuuming. When she's finished, she props the vacuum against the chair and hauls the tub of stuff to her old bedroom. She lies on the bed. Ginny has moved the dresser and the bed around, and now it looks like a hotel. Even the faces in her photo frames look generic. How long ago did she know these people? Right now, everyone is milling around the table, she knows. They're hungry. They are running out of things to say. She takes her sweet time. There is a letter Jack gave her in high school. She keeps it with others in her Bible, in the drawer of this childhood nightstand. Ginny could walk in to read them any old time. So could Frank, but he wouldn't. Hazel unfolds it from its tight little packet and skims it, down to the bottom. Jack wrote, *. . . so pure the whitest snow looks filthy next to you.* She lets the letter rest on her just-rounded belly and wonders what's wrong with her.

*

Ginny tells Jack he'd better wash his hands before he eats. "All that old dust," she says, shaking her head. And who knows what he's picked up in the shed? It's a legitimate ruse and he has to get out, at least for a minute or two. While he's gone, Ginny goes to the corner cabinet with Frank and takes out two bottles—Frank's medicine. One is a clear liquid that he has to take with a tablespoon. The other, capsules. He takes two at each meal with a full glass of water. She knows she doesn't have to do this for him, doesn't have to guide the tablespoon into his mouth. But his hand shakes so. As if he has the medicine to be afraid of and nothing else.

The roast is beautiful: sliced, pink, and marbled with fat. There are peeled potatoes in the roaster, and carrots, thickly salted and peppered. A thick, greasy broth pools around. There is bread from the store on both ends, still in plastic bags, and tubs of butter. A big boat of brown gravy and more warming on the stove. It's nothing fancy. They could all make juicy sandwiches, if they wanted to. And Hazel probably will, she decides, when she comes out of her room and takes a look at the spread. The bread will turn soggy, and she'll dip each bite in a pool of gravy. The strings of meat catching between her teeth, her sucking at them. Her nausea has passed. They can't eat soon enough.

Jack comes out from the bathroom and wipes his hands on his jeans. Hazel kisses his cheek, leans into him. It is so unexpected, affectionate. Jack can't help but run his hand down her front most tenderly, his hand lingering on the swell where she used to tuck in her shirts. He kneels down as if they are alone in the room, and even when they are alone in the room, this bothers her—the way he cradles her belly with two spread hands and kisses it full on. Hazel runs her hands through his hair.

But then Hazel is pulling his head away from her. She says, loudly, "It's just a spill." She fans her shirt as if it's wet.

Why lie right up to the last minute? Jack wonders what would be a better way to tell her parents than right now, in this rare moment when they've forgotten themselves? He and Hazel will have to forget themselves, lose themselves, more every day. That is what the child grows on. He looks up at her and wonders if he could plant this selflessness in her if he stared at her deeply enough. She deceives so easily.

Ginny closes the corner cabinet. She grabs a towel and runs cold water over it, soaking the tip. She rushes over and pushes it up against a spot that, Jack realizes, really is on the front of Hazel's shirt. But it is an old spot. Ginny, too, is putting on an act. Now everyone knows about the baby, but everyone will act as if they don't know. That is the way this family works: secret piled on secret. Hazel looks up at the ceiling while they bend over her belly. Ginny rubs at the spot. She murmurs to Jack, "I just hope it hasn't set."

Frank, still in the corner, doesn't know who is to be pitied more: the child or these clueless parents, who are too frightened to admit a thing. God willing, the birth will be difficult, and they'll be stripped of their resources, their airs—then they can move on to something deeper. He and Ginny have just entered into a kind of honeymoon. At night, he sits at one end of the sofa with the leg rest kicked up, and a little cup of wine on the stand next to him. Ginny lies along the couch's length. She props her back up with pillows and rests her feet in Frank's lap. The TV is off. He rubs her socked feet—he has never done this before—and can't get enough of rubbing them. The great swoops of bone, the fineness. Ginny reads aloud to him, the book resting in her lap. She reads, *You have not come to something that can be touched, a blazing fire, and darkness, and gloom, and a tempest, and the sound of a trumpet. . . .*

Frank tells her stories. He didn't know how many stories he had to tell until he started spilling them out. How, when he was seventeen and leaving for the military, he climbed up a tree and said goodbye to every living thing he saw—the rabbits, the deer, the squirrel that climbed up next to Frank and, from the shock of seeing Frank, fell back out of the tree, into the snow . . . *and a voice whose words made the hearers beg that not another word be spoken to them.* But Frank came back to it all: the woods, the house, the people. Now, whenever he walks past that tree, he pushes his palm against the bark as if to soak in the memory all over again.

And Ginny, at the end of the couch, keeps shaking her head and saying, "I didn't know. I didn't know what all you had in there." Had in there, had in him.

"It's fine," Hazel says, and swats their hands away. "It's nothing to cry over." She takes the towel out of Ginny's hands and drops it on the table, next to her place. Everyone is staring at her. Even her father, and Hazel knows he can't stand the petting Ginny and Jack can get into. She straightens the front of her shirt. If only there was a way that the cold wet wouldn't hit her skin, but the shirt is just not big enough. She fishes her hand into one of the bread bags and grabs a slice. With her knife, she slathers on a thick layer of butter, which is warm from sitting out, and she slathers a thick layer on. "Are we ready?" she asks. She shows some restraint and sets the bread on the edge of her plate. She licks her fingers. "I can't last much longer."

They sit. Ginny bows her head over her plate. "Hazel," she says. Hazel stares at her. Her panic is obvious, like a smell. The rest have dodged it, the praying, this time. Jack lays his hands out to Hazel and Ginny. Frank, across the table, does the same. Ginny's hand is warm and dry, chapped from dishwater. *You have not come to something that can be touched.* That's what Ginny read. And now Frank says goodbye to the hands gliding over varnished wood and softened leather. The times he has slid his finger in front of a trigger while the fall sun spotted the grass between the leaves. Cupping water from the pump. Twisting rope, tying twine string, braiding wire just to hold it all together, to hold it in. To hold things back. *You have not come.* The bruises, the nicks of his everyday work. His whiskered face rubbing against Ginny's soft cheek, morning after morning.

"Hazel—pray," Frank says. He takes her damp hand. The roast steams. They all bow their heads.

III.

At the schoolhouse, there are six students. They range in age from seven to fourteen. Frank is the oldest. They have their desks huddled near the pot-bellied stove. It is mid-April, 1952, and an epic blizzard has let itself loose. The morning had been mild. The students had walked to class wearing light jackets or flannel shirts. No one wore boots. The teacher stopped talking some time ago. She paces from the east window to the west. Frank does not notice the teacher or the snow. He thinks only of the night before, swearing up and down to his father and mother that he hadn't done it, he hadn't done a thing to the tire. There was no paying for the repair for another month, at least. They'd have to drive the horses. "The horses!" his brother had snorted.

"And if this causes any trouble," his father said to Frank, "you'll be getting it."

The teacher turns. She calls off class. The students cheer and gather their slates. The chalk dusts their shirtsleeves. They are gone. The teacher is maybe eighteen. She tells Frank to take care of the fire and go home. Her boots echo across the floorboards. She wraps herself up in her shawl, shivers, and leaves.

Frank sits with the fire. The logs burn down. The few worksheets tossed in go fast. Frank is in no hurry to get home. He knocks the wood, and when it collapses on itself, he rakes it down until it's all ash and coals.

Outside, it is a whiteout. He slips on the stoop and slides clear down the four steps. The snow is thick and sloppy. When he gets his footing, he takes a sharp right and has to drag his legs along behind him. The drifts eat up the road. They come past his knees. His jeans and socks are soaked. He walks. The snow sticks to him and he feels invisible. So this is what it is to disappear, he thinks. Cold. Difficult in a way that makes trying pointless. It is a two-mile walk home. There is a great desire to just lie in the snow and wait for the dogs to find him once it's melted. He would be covered with flowers.

And then there are bells, and as the bells jingle closer, Frank thinks he is dreaming. That this is all a dream—he'd just fallen asleep sitting too close to the fire in class. The horses come, the pair of them, and his father stands behind them on the front of the sled, leaning back with the reins. "Whoa," his father says, deeply, and the horses slow. "Whoa." His father does not look at Frank. On the back of the sled are his brother and his sister, picked up from the high school in town.

"Get up. Come on," his brother calls. He sits on the sled bed, his arms spread out along the rail, wearing nothing but a collar shirt as if it wasn't cold. His sister stands and helps Frank in. In Frank's memory, his sister is flitting around like an angel, dressed in a white gown. But, of course, she is no angel. Before the horses take off again, she slaps her hand over their brother's mouth. Their brother is saying, "You ruined everything, Frank. It was either getting you or bringing the cows in. The cows are probably toast—udders bursting. I could have got you with the car two hours ago if—"

And Frank looks up at his father and sees, out of his back pants pocket, the strap of the blackjack hanging out. Frank starts whispering, praying, everything gentle and kind—he feels the bruises growing already, growing along his forearms and shins—he pleads and asks, and the horses are shaking the sled back home.

His sister goes to him and wipes away his tears. In his memory, she too cannot feel the cold. "We'll have a ham," she says, "that'll warm us up. And we'll listen to *The Shadow* and drink hot cider with nutmeg and cinnamon, and mother will pop corn on the stove. Boy," she says, and Frank does not stop shaking his head, "are we ever going to have a good time."

Let the Rivers Clap Their Hands

At eighteen, Theresa saw her grandmother trying to escape Alzheimer's, only to get struck by, then sucked under, a bus. Since then, Theresa clings to details, absurdities, people. A *Newsweek* article said that in order to avoid Alzheimer's, the best strategy was to grow as many brain synapses as possible. Don't do the same things over and over again. Don't say the same things over and over again. Snappy syntax is a must. *Dendrites save lives. Clichés will kill you like a bus. Brush your teeth with your dominant hand to save your gums. Brush your teeth with your weak hand to save your granddaughter from a life of torment.* These would be her mottos, if she wasn't too terrified to repeat them.

She clings to Jack, and in the night, Jack has given up on sleep. The next two weeks are looming large. Weeks when he will be on the road, for one thing. And weeks when Theresa will be nannying a friend's child. *Nannying,* he wants to say. *Don't you think it's too soon after?* But he can't bring himself to say it. He wonders if he should even have to say it. He tries to focus on the morning run that won't happen: Crisp air in his lungs. Pine trees breaking through gray skies. The rubbery kneecap snap, back and front. And his mind—a happy blank. Instead he sees all those puddles he will have to jump through just to get to his car, and the washed-out gravel, and the trees blown over.

He breathes and pushes all those night thoughts away, and with them that morning three months ago: the way Theresa's body panted like a dog, the way she screamed like something was being torn out of her, because it was, and the way the baby hung there, silent, in the doctor's slippery hands.

But here are the hands, Theresa's, clutching him.

"I dreamt I was a bomb," she whispers. "I destroyed everything."

Jack folds the covers down and leads her to the kitchen, where she sits on their ripped vinyl chair, her upper body draped on the table, her cheek on the Formica. She stares at the scotch, which Jack has not diluted this time, and her eyes follow the shadowy pattern of flowers that the etched tumbler casts around the room. She sits up and drinks. Jack leans against the countertop. He sees Theresa as she is: a mess of brown hair, a heap of clothes, a puffy face. He knows that, since the baby, these are the terms she has come to associate with herself, whom neither of them recognizes. Her daily speech has taken on the nuanced mumble of subway traffic, confused and sedated—slowing with *What's the point?* and coming to a full stop with *I have no point.*

Now, as she tells him about her dream, he can see the panic in her eyes. She clasps her head and tells him about the sound like a mosquito trapped in her ear and the air pressing on her as she traveled through the sky, how it felt like she was shrinking rapidly, the air wrenched out of her, her skin flaking off like shingles. And through it all, the slow motion feeling of disaster with which she's so familiar. Then bang. Everything destroyed. The city looks like crumpled wrapping paper spread over the carpet on Christmas morning.

When she finishes, she is crying. "I always wanted a Christmas that looked like that." She looks to Jack for answers he doesn't have. He dreads these sentences that run out of her mouth in the night. They're like silk scarves pulled by a magician, scarves that become crows when thrown into the air, and hover overhead.

*

These are the days of the five-hundred-year flood, a term the insurance companies have come to curse for its inaccuracy. This is the third such flood the area has suffered in two decades. The homeowners and farmers who removed their flood insurance after the first, not expecting another deluge for 499 years, pound the insurers' phone lines down. They want answers, or at least some money. Crop damages run over fifty million. Everything exposed to the weather blown in from the west is demolished. Trees, swing sets, struck down nightly. Fields of corn and oats are laid waste, shredded into ribbons by hail, abandoned, corrupted, in fields that are now swamp. The stench pushes the farmers back into their beds, under the blankets, unable to grasp what it is they should do with food that has decayed, still milky in its husk.

What is not ravaged by hail and lightning and water is covered with mildew. The towns are rotting away, from the river up. Baseball games are purgatoried into *not happening tonight anyway.*

A herd of cattle is flushed downriver. It is Biblical: a pastoral psalm gone wrong, a herd of swine suddenly taking on the people's demons and hurling itself over a cliff. But this is an image of grace: the many bobbing white heads, the cows and their calves, always so calm. The soft lowing over the gurgle of water. If only all exorcisms could be so gentle.

*

Theresa calls this house "The Ark." She says it seems a person should feel safe inside it. The house belongs to Jack's parents, Herb and Margaret. They thrive on this kind of compliment, and Theresa is full of them. But Margaret still isn't sure what her son is doing with a jittery flake of a girl like her. She feels she could melt the girl down to a teardrop just by standing too close. And so, she's kept her distance and shushed Theresa out of the kitchen, secretly hoping her son will move on.

The house is one of the few places to have survived with no damage. This is a source of pride for Margaret. They designed the house themselves (correction: herself) and built it on the highest hill they could find in town. Margaret has taken to throwing her hands up in the air whenever Theresa mentions it. She acts as if she had nothing to do with it, saying, "It's as if God himself had given us the plans!" She feels favored. He knows this.

The house is large, a three-story with vaulted ceilings and windows so wide and tall they take the whole of the Mississippi Valley and bring it in. Jack stands near the window, his outstretched hand moving over the cliff and the rushing current. Margaret, chopping potatoes for lunch, knows that Jack is showing his father—her good-natured husband—the changing landscape. Jack, a geologist with the university, is working overtime, studying the new currents and unearthed caves, the sudden springs this weather has brought on. But Margaret doesn't see her good-natured husband when she looks up. She doesn't see Theresa, either, though she is sure to be lurking nearby. She sees her son, his strong-chinned profile darkened by the sun shining in, claiming all this land as his own with the slightest motion of his hand. The lost child was upsetting, but not overly so. It was almost expected.

After they eat ribs and potato salad, the four of them mill around the house: small talk, paint swatches, dirty dishes. The TV is flipped on—golf, baseball. Eventually they congregate near the window and look down at the valley. It is hard not to look at, like a pile-up along the highway or a hook where someone's hand used to be. The tricky part is not getting involved: running off the road, offending with a stare. But here, now, it seems safe to look. Herb says, "All that flooding doesn't bother us any. Look at it. It only gives us more of that river to enjoy. A man can't be angry about that." Margaret nods along.

The tops of trailers and the peaks of new homes built along the river pop up through the widened current. A man poles a canoe. He pushes off against a chimney, heading for land.

*

Main Street is a steep hill. At the top, the storefronts are blown out. The broken glass that was not washed away in the night is settled in the street. It reflects what remains of the neon signs: *Open, Bud Lite, Fresh Cheese Curds.* The owner of the liquor store sits on his stool behind the register, a broom laid across his lap. On the floor are toppled wine racks and burst bottles in puddles of violet and burgundy. The pale, untreated wood will be stained. His wife told him not to stack the good wine near the window. Thieves, she said. But no, he said, he will. It's classy. It pulls the money in: the insurance salesmen, lawyers, a doctor or two—all tourists. Six-packs can put a roof over your head. Malbec and Champagne can put a pool in your yard, or first, attach a yard to your house. He bends and dips his finger in it, wanting to get a taste of what he has only sold. He puts his finger to his mouth and sucks. No matter how he cleans this floor, his customers will be greeted with this stain for as long as he can keep the shop running. The beer, safe in coolers along the back wall, will be sold out by the end of the day.

Down the street, the mayor wears flip-flops and a T-shirt because he is at work: students carry armfuls of soggy books from the library and load them into truck beds. The water hits just above the knee, the lower thigh—that area the Catholic schoolboys' eyes have skimmed across for so many years, in this very library, while attempting homework. What was once erotic is now common: the wet T-shirts, the clinging pants. A hand on the back consoles, instead of searching for the zipper.

Mosquitoes breed in the new still pools and take their fill.

The books drip and flop over the workers' forearms just like the sandbags with which the town has grown familiar, and, like anything familiar, cursed for being worthless. Pages fall from spines and coat the water. They wind their way through the streets and head downriver. A TV crew is there for an interview.

"We are trying to salvage everything," the mayor says, "but this is madness. This is inescapable."

*

Enter Seth. Three years old, running across the lawn in a garbage-bag cape. His feet, no larger than decks of cards, slosh through muddy water, ankle-deep. "Tornado! It's a tornado coming!" he shouts, spinning clumsily, arms out, and topples over into Theresa's lap.

Seth is on loan for two weeks. Or, put another way: his parents went on vacation. Theresa has heard nothing from Sheila for months, and now she has her son. Sheila has told Theresa the following about the boy: preschool has made him paranoid. He comes home certain that mosquito bites will kill him, that strangers will pluck him from his parents' arms and force him to clean chimneys (*I don't even know* how *to clean chimneys!* he sometimes adds, mid-sob), that any bag of M&M's could be filled with pills instead of chocolate. He wants desperately to know what *die* means, what it really means.

"It will be good practice for you and Jack," Sheila said, and winked at Theresa.

It wasn't until late that night that Theresa realized: Sheila never knew Theresa had been pregnant.

Back in this moment, Seth is running, toppling. The backs of his legs are speckled with mud his feet have kicked up. They are in Margaret and Herb's yard. Jack's parents are bleary-eyed in their lawn chairs. They say it's only the humidity—"It just gets us down." They sip drinks—Margaret a Bloody Mary, Herb a martini. Theresa suspects Margaret is trying to drink away the two weeks that Theresa will be staying there with a stranger's child. On top of that, Jack will be gone, traveling, for most of it. Theresa doesn't care. She feels she needs to be watched. After all, what does she know about children that could keep one alive? Herb slaps at a mosquito on his leg, and then, as if that effort were too great, lazily waves at another on his arm.

Seth turns his head in Theresa's lap. He asks where the tornado is.

"There is no tornado," she says. "Look." She points up. "There's the sun. Tornados don't come out in the sun." And then she can't help it. She kisses the fat tops of his white feet, her hair falling down and around. She wipes muddy water away with her thumb.

"No," he says, and grabs her arm. He is frustrated. He believes she has misunderstood him. He rephrases, asks: "But is a tornado gonna come and take me away?" Theresa shakes her head. She wishes there were a better way to reassure him. But as far as she can tell, he only needs to see it not happen for as long as possible—until he forgets he is afraid, or until a tornado comes and takes him away. From her grandmother's house, Theresa was able to hear the coal trains as they passed. Whenever she heard the whistle blowing, she took off for the porch, sure the train would jump track, that it was coming into the yard to run her down.

Seth takes off again, twirling past Herb and Margaret. He has a way of tilting his head all the way back and smiling, closed-eyed, when he twirls. He looks like a blind man dancing.

And then he crumples right in front of them. His head falls to one side as if Theresa has just slapped him and he doesn't understand why. So much so, Theresa wonders if this has happened, if she has slapped him. "Ow," he whispers, the red rushing to his face. She moves to him, kneels in the puddle beside him. She doesn't know where to look. Her fingers flit over his body, flip his arms for bee stings. He shakes her hands off his arm.

Margaret shouts over Theresa's shoulder, "Look at his foot, woman." There, embedded in the pad of his foot, is the broken top of a glass bottle, debris blown in from last night's storm.

"It's okay," Theresa says. She doesn't want to pull the glass out yet. That's when the blood will come. "It's fine."

Margaret stands. "What?" She says, "You want it to get infected? Move it."

"Infected?" Seth says. He pulls his leg up, looks at the green glass buried in it, the color building up under the skin. "It's gonna fall off!" he says and looks up at Margaret. He reaches down and pulls the glass out. Blood comes with it.

He shouts at Theresa, "My foot's gonna fall off!" She can't think. "Who told you that?" she asks. It keeps bleeding. She shoves the palm of her hand into the cut. "Who told you that?" She looks up to Margaret, expecting her to do something.

But Margaret is watching Herb, who has just realized his drink has been knocked over. He spies an olive, speared with a toothpick, floating in a puddle. He struggles to get out of the lawn chair, to bend and pick the olive from the puddle. He studies it. When he sees it is inedible, he throws the olive into his now-empty glass and heads back to the house.

That night, the storms plow through again. In bed, Theresa runs her hands over her feet, her legs, checking for cuts.

When the tornado siren goes off, she carries Seth to the basement. They sit in the crawlspace, wrapped in blankets. She gives him a flashlight, and he dances the beam around the room and into their eyes until they see colors.

*

Seth's questions stretch on. "Are there bees out here? Where did Herb's hair go? Why did somebody steal your bike when you were a little girl? Is somebody gonna steal my bike?" Theresa answers them as best she can, a mixture of honesty and distraction. She says, "I think that's just what happens when you forget things: they get snatched away. Like your ears. When was the last time you remembered your ears?" Seth brings a hand to the side of his face, slowly, as if afraid of what he'll discover. Theresa quickly pinches his earlobe and pulls her hand away as if she's grabbed it. Seth brushes her arm away and smiles. But he is never distracted for long.

*

Through the week, the TV stations play this clip: A train approaches a flooded river valley in Iowa and slows, slows. Its change in direction is slight at first, then becomes obvious. Boys standing by the water's edge in baseball uniforms run from the tracks. The water rushes up to their knees and higher, slowing them. Behind, the train curls slowly off the track, slinking, like a caterpillar going in for a drink. Coal tumbles off the carts as they tip down and level off, disappearing into the water. The boys are safe—but as the water recedes, it tugs, and they are pulled in, closer to the wreck. Already-rotted siding is ripped off homes, and floats. The engine driver escapes and clings to the boards. He kicks his way to land.

Theresa sees this in her dreams but in them, she is there, and Seth is in her arms, his head buried in her shoulder. Her back presses against a wall of limestone and the wave of water travels up, beyond her hips. She allows the waves to pull her legs forward—it's so easy, just a few steps—before she forces herself awake.

Jack is kissing her neck, touching her thigh. She slips out of bed and pulls on her bathrobe. She walks down the hall and into Seth's room. He is sucking his thumb, his pajama sleeve wrapped around his fist. He wakes and pulls his thumb out of his mouth long enough to say, "You're layin' with me?" and puts the thumb back in. Theresa nods and lies down. She settles her head on the pillow beside him. They sleep.

*

It's Saturday, a better day, Jack thinks. He's not working. Theresa is in the kitchen, cutting meat and vegetables for a stew. What is left over, she is placing in gallon-sized plastic bags. Jack sits at the kitchen table, flipping through the paper. He can't remember the last time Theresa cooked.

Seth stands close to Theresa. He is pointing to everything, the vegetables, the spices, asking why this is cut that way, why she's putting those dried leaves in there. Jack is amazed. They seem like a perfect match, like the siblings neither one has.

Theresa gives Seth a dried oregano leaf to taste, and he puts it on his tongue, pursing and smacking his lips to dramatize the tasting. He does a dance, bouncing side to bandaged side while he does it. It is a good day.

"Hey. Why're you wrapping all that up?" Seth asks.

"You know," Theresa says. "To keep it fresh. So I can keep it for a long time."

"Hey." Seth turns and throws his hands up. "I got an idea—you should keep *me* fresh." He points to his chest, and in the same moment, Theresa says, "Wonderful idea," grabs a new plastic bag from the box, and fits it over his head. They are both laughing. Seth grabs the sides of the bag and pulls it tight against his face. His nose is flat like a pig's and Theresa rubs her own against it and they both laugh some more. Jack stands. "Theresa," he says. "Stop."

She turns and stares at Jack. He can tell she doesn't get it. Then she traces her arms, her hands, back to Seth's head, and he is beginning to gasp. She rips the bag off his head, out of his hands. She throws the bag on the stove and the plastic melts onto the burner. She turns to Seth. "Never do that again. Understand me? Never."

She turns and leaves the kitchen. Jack moves Seth away from the stove. He pushes the knives left out on the countertop to the wall. Seth starts to cry, and Jack lifts him up to his shoulder. He looks out the window and sees Theresa pacing on the porch. Her mouth moves. She is talking to herself. Jack is glad he can't hear what she's saying.

*

A tornado goes through Iowa in the night. A Boy Scout troop stays in the woods. The camp is hit. The cabin's walls, the roof, are sucked away and blown out into the trees. The boys are left with the concrete floor, their heads covered, trying to cling on to one another: legs and arms attempting to latch. The bunk beds collapse and the wood and mattresses are dodged or hidden under—no one knows what to do.

Four boys are taken, gone. All the boys are injured. On national television, a reporter interviews a survivor and his parents. The boy is barely as tall as his father's waist and is draped in a black garbage bag to protect him from the rain. In the background, the trees are flattened. Khaki clothing torn, thrown about.

The TV is switched off.

*

The storms continue to march through. The president declares the entire Midwest a disaster area and promises funds will come soon. Each morning, in one way or another, the feature news story is the flood: A tree has fallen onto a woman's house, and her child is killed. Riverfront businesses are whisked away, and jobs lost. Communities are on the verge of becoming ghost towns. Corn production is down, eliminated, and the price of groceries skyrockets. Gas, too. A dam bursts in Wisconsin and a lake disappears. So do homes. There are no tourists. Residents are arrested: insanity, stabbings, looting.

Throughout town, unheard-of water sources continue to appear. The water table rises so high that geysers emerge from hillsides. The river is no longer the only culprit. In the few moments between storms and tornados, when a temporary lull was once enjoyed, the earth appears to be sobbing, worn out.

The floor of St. Thomas Church cracks in the center, the pattern of the crack radiating like that of a window hit by a bullet. A spring emerges from the crack, and water shoots up past the height of the pews. The TV crew takes in the crucifix, Mary, the saints, finally the spring and the priest. "We don't know what to make of this," the priest says. He, too, is afraid to speak. Is this a miracle or a warning?

*

Theresa wakes to thunder. It is past midnight. She pads down the hall and turns on the TV. The weather map is clotted with red and orange. Counties are listed. The weatherman is interrupted continually with more warnings of floods, thunderstorms, tornados. Theresa turns the volume up and walks down to Seth's room. She whispers to him, pulls his thumb from his mouth, and guides him out of bed. He grabs the flashlight from the nightstand.

On their way downstairs, Margaret steps out of her bedroom, arms crossed over her nightdress, and whispers loudly, "What's all this?"

"Come downstairs," Theresa says, and keeps walking.

The basement is lit from the lightning strikes shining through the windows. The carpet is wet. It jars them both. In her mind, Theresa can see loose electrical wires snaking their way through the walls, heading for the water. Seth lifts his arms out to her, and she picks him up and carries him to the crawlspace under the stairs.

They hear Margaret and Herb coming down. From where Theresa sits with Seth, it sounds like many more people. "Oh my God," Margaret says. She turns on the lights. Theresa looks out the door.

There is water falling in where the ceiling and the wall meet. It is running down in sheets. There is no crack, no open window. It is coming, it seems, from nowhere.

Margaret runs upstairs and comes back with a pile of towels. She throws them on the floor. “My carpet,” she whispers. She and Herb roll the towels and line the floor along the walls. But the carpet is already wet through, and the storm is not letting up. Margaret begins to wipe the walls, gently, like she would a child’s face. She takes hold of Herb’s arm and teaches him the motion.

Seth stands at the crawlspace door, watching this, confused, until Theresa pulls him back in. “Come on,” she says. It is still dry in here, for a few more minutes at least. She and Seth sit bundled in blankets. She twirls the flashlight around and around the small space. The beam dances across the walls. Seth’s eyes follow the revolutions the light makes, and it is like many short days are going by in their world, and they are remaining warm and dry and safe.

Circumstances

It was settled, then. A fog had gathered in the streets overnight. Hazel reached across the driver's seat and put the last bag on the passenger side. Fruit and hard-boiled eggs and a jelly jar with water, that was all.

Someone she knew had died in Wisconsin. It didn't matter who, as she wouldn't make the services, but it did matter—death had visited. So, she was leaving Smith and leaving Miami. Miami had not fit anyway. The whole sun-blown show. Last week, someone had drowned in a public bathhouse. She and Smith had often gone there and could not get in past the ambulances that day. Her ancestors had not emigrated from Bohemia so that she could sweat in a bathhouse, networking, detoxifying, getting centered—whatever. She was glad she would never see the place again.

Smith had proposed on Sunday. He'd found the ring in a sock while she was packing. "I've had this ring for two years," he said. It was amazing, the rate at which forgotten and misplaced things accrue. She'd often forgotten they were a couple at all.

"Oh, sure," she had said. "Now hand me that pillow. Otherwise these cups might as well shatter in my hands."

It was early—still dark. Her car half on, half off the sidewalk. Smith loomed over her. He futzed, one-handed, with what he could. In the other hand, he had the dog by her leash. When the car was packed, Hazel turned to him. Then she turned away and patted the dog on her head. "Well," she said. Smith bent to kiss her. That was when the dog jerked loose and ran down the street. The dog's tags jangled into the mist. Smith ran after her. "Goodbye!" Hazel called. It was better this way. A taxicab honked. Hazel turned off her hazard lights and pulled out.

*

She stopped on the far side of Atlanta. The room was more than she could afford. There was a restaurant off the lobby with white napkins and crystal, but she bought a microwave dinner from the incidental shop—something, the least offensive. Before the bedroom was another room with couches and a desk. The space made her uncomfortable, so she pulled a chair over and angled it under the door handle. It would not stop anyone, but it would, at least, make noise. She ate the microwave dinner in her room while sitting on her bed and looked at the dresser that likely opened up into a TV. It was still daylight. She took a long shower and was careless with the towels. They lay damp on the tile, the short-scrub carpet. She hung one from her neck the way a man would and didn't bother dressing. She leaned against the pillows and watched hours of TV. It bored her, and her mind wandered, but she knew others watched it and so she did, to have something to talk about when she got back. It seemed she'd not had a night alone in years.

*

Hazel spent the next night in Cincinnati with an old friend. As she pulled into his driveway, she wondered if this was the real reason for the trip—not because death had visited, but because she missed this sad friend. Her time in Cincinnati had been brief—a few feral months in a near-empty apartment. She had paced the floorboards, made desperate phone calls, applied facial masks, and sat with her legs propped against the wall so the blood would flow to her head and fix her. She bought strange warehouse goods, Goodwill chairs, coffee cups, picture frames to fill the spaces, only to donate them back weeks later. It was a cheap hobby. This friend had calmed her, or so she had thought. Or so she had heard some former beau say about women—that they calmed him. That had been his excuse. This Cincinnati friend had frequently answered her phone calls. At the time, he felt like a miracle.

As she left Cincinnati, she thought that she did not miss Miami, but she did miss interesting people. Her next stop would be her last—her destination. It had been a long time since she'd reached one of those.

*

The new apartment was the bottom floor of an old house. A historic landmark, was what the advertisement said. A governor had lived there in the late 1800s. The landlord was late to meet her—an old friend of his had died. It was a wet summer and the trees spread, luscious. She sat on the steps until she decided to walk around the house and see how easily it could be broken into. Very. There were low, open windows with dense bushes underneath. It smelled like fresh paint. She looked in and saw a fan oscillating back and forth on the kitchen counter, ruffling papers held under a coffee cup. As if someone had already been here, someone like her father, who might have decided to drive down for a day, to make sure the place checked out, and while there written a list of repairs that weren't necessary but would be nice. That's how it was with him in the end. Another person altogether.

The landlord showed up in a suit that sloped off his shoulders. The cuffs went to his knuckles. She wouldn't have noticed something like this if she hadn't lived in Miami and been judged harshly for these same things. Hazel wrote two checks. Only one wall had been painted a dark red, which made her believe something horrible had happened there. A fly buzzed around the landlord's head. He swatted at it until Hazel saw a new look come across his face: he reached out and grabbed the fly from the air.

"This has never happened before," he said. "Never. What are the chances it happens today?"

Hazel was not sure what today meant to him, aside from it being his friend's funeral, so she smiled. She was determined to make this place work for the long haul.

"I hope this isn't so, but it seems I cough these days, and one of these flies out. I talk, and there's a gnat. Do you think that's medically possible?"

"I'm sorry for your loss."

"Oh? Oh. He was my father's pastor. When I was young, he always tugged on my ears. I think he meant to pull quarters from them."

Hazel walked around the little place and flipped the light switches on and off. She tried the faucets.

"You know," the landlord said, "I think that's the only reason I stayed in town. Someone was always just about to die. Mother always told us that we'd leave her to die like a dog in some home." He wiped his nose with his suit sleeve and switched off the fan. "I had to prove her wrong." He raised his fist to his face—it had been clenched this whole time—and opened it with a flourish. The fly shot out. "Would you look at that?"

*

Christmastime, and the snow was falling in clusters. Hazel was driving home from the grade school holiday program. Her niece and nephew, the two who belonged to Liz, had sung. Her niece, the younger of the two, had taken Hazel's hand and led her around her classroom, to point out her painted Rudolph and her desk, her graham cracker house with the jimmy-speckled roofline. She had flashed her underpants at a boy when she thought Hazel wasn't looking.

"I hate that kid," her niece had said, then skipped down the hallway and knocked a red bulb from the tree. It shattered quietly beside the tree's quilted skirt. Hazel had neglected these children, and she often felt there was no stopping them.

Hazel took the back way home, past a feed mill and a farm that advertised fresh frying chickens. A salt truck passed her going the other way. A beagle wearing a Christmas bow ran beside it and barked at the truck's groaning. She hardly noticed when she slid off the road and into a ditch.

*

Liz had insisted for some years now that Hazel has let her circumstances control her life, instead of the other way around. At-home mothers were filled with this sort of wisdom. Liz listened to audiobooks while dusting and maintained a yoga practice for the sake of her family. There were framed mantras to read while sitting at both table and toilette. Liz also told Hazel that she was praying for the right man to come along. "It's the most obvious solution, and I just don't get it. I don't get it," she would repeat, and look off thoughtfully while her son spit cookie into the garbage behind her. Hazel's nephew had what was called a texture issue. "Why didn't you make the plain ones?" he would ask.

Besides the ditch, there were other accidents—a twisted ankle, an apartment break-in, one ovarian cyst—that affected Hazel more than they would have affected others. She had so few means for coping. She was a bank teller and not full-time at that. She often felt one paper cut away from homelessness. She gave blood regularly under the belief that it reduced her blood pressure. Afterward, she would sit on her couch for hours, staring. Now that she was in a ditch, she would have to call her sister to send her husband, who would reluctantly help Hazel. It was an old story by now, and she had lived here for only a year and a half. Hazel turned on her hazard lights and considered sitting there until morning. Then she checked the gas gauge and killed the engine.

A long line of cars drove past her, slowly and carefully—all merry, she was sure. This road was usually dead, which was why she preferred it. Someone pulled behind her. The headlights caught her mirrors, and then the hazards came on. Likely her sister's family, her brother-in-law thrilled to have caught her early. Feeling he had beaten Hazel at her own game.

But it was not them. Her brother-in-law was no detective. He did not notice whether the cookies were plain or otherwise, he simply chewed.

Hazel licked her lips and prepared something self-effacing to say—that would be the responsible tone here. Light from passing cars caught the steam from a man's mouth as he walked toward her. The walk was stupid and hunched, so she was glad for the outline of a wife in the rearview mirror, happy to see the car seat. Whatever happened in the next five minutes would not have to last beyond tonight—no reason to be endlessly, adulterously thankful. What has happened to her that her mind goes to these places, these extremes? A better question might be, what hasn't happened to her? She cranked down the window and there was Jack, blue-eyed and beautiful, with snow in his hair. Beside him, Hazel had been a handsome woman—that had been her joke for a while.

"I recognized your license plate," he said.

"Of course." He said the plainest things. "I just—drifted off." She made a motion with her hand, and with this motion she meant to account for the ice, her mood, the circumstances. It was dark, and he didn't see her gesture.

"You shouldn't drink so much."

The beagle that had been running with the plow had given up and trotted home. The bow had fallen to his puppy waist and it dragged against the snow. The dog scratched at the bow with his stubby hind leg. It was pointless, so pointless to argue with Jack. One New Year, she resolved never to do it again, and twenty days into January, she left him.

"I was at the Christmas program," she said. She had seen him there, talking to the priest about birdwatching, the winter berries, pumpkin seeds, laughing and endearing himself, as always, to the powerful. To think she had been with this man for twenty years, from ages ten to twenty to thirty and more—no, to think even that she'd been alive—alive in the manner she had been—for that long, and more—longer, it was enough to make her want to die. Failure. A snail's death, something small and coiled. *Hazel is always so easily discouraged*—something her mother had said. *If she doesn't get it right the first time, she just quits.* Her mother had tried, and it has taken years for Hazel to admit this.

"Of all the places." He said it with a sneer. It was to be expected.

Hazel said, "Someone's on his way." She watched his expression for the twitch. Then he looked over his shoulder, into the headlights of all those passing cars. Each parishioner and parent recognizing him and praising Jack for his goodness, his incredible patience. *With that woman,* tacked on for those in the know. "Which means," Hazel said, "you can go."

"I'm looking at it," he finally decided. "You'll freeze before he gets here. Whoever."

He opened the door, and like a good child, she got out. Broken ice crunched under her boots—so rubbery and fur-lined and regrettable. The boots made her look like a drag. But what did it matter here in Wisconsin? Why not be a drag? Along this side of the road there was a cornfield, which in winter meant delicate rows of snow as far as Hazel could see, until the horizon became black-blue—deep nothing. In the Jeep behind her, Theresa—the wife—turned on the dome light. She waved at Hazel and motioned for her to come in. Hazel had never seen her look so beautiful. The cold had left her cheeks pink and the light made her hair seem shiny, though it was not, and it never had been.

The homes across the street were bedecked with strings of hanging white lights, bursted bulbs, blank strands. The beagle sat and looked in a house window. Between cars passing by was a holiday melody, electronic and flat. She'd surrounded herself with such cheap life. What a choice to move back into it. She had never experienced happiness here. She said this sometimes, and no one believed her. Simple nights walking with Jack along deserted streets, feeling frozen and gentle. Even those she'd misspent. Cars passed, rusted and white with salt. Slush flew up, waist high. Someone honked and honked again and slowed. She felt she was in a position where she could go neither forward nor backward—she had been both places—and so she stared at the Christmas lights until she felt she was deep in something like prayer. But she knew she was only building her own selfish drama.

The honking car stopped in the road and the passenger-side window rolled down. "I thought it was you," the priest called to her. His athletic jacket was zipped to his chin, and his lips, his ears—all had grown round and voluptuous, greased against the cold. This lonely man, poor in spirit. Cars idled behind him. No one would honk because it was the priest. "I thought I saw a ghost. I mean, in the school, I thought I saw your mother." He leaned over the passenger seat and looked at her as if he were checking yet again. When Hazel was young, he had gone through a phase where he would lift her ponytail and neigh. "It was just you," he finally said. "What brings you back now? Your parents were just—well, your mother always thought—"

Hazel looked at the line of cars behind him, recognized the faces, knew the conversation: "Where else would I be?" she said. There were certain phrases she said repeatedly, normal dialogue that made her want to sob.

"What seems to be the problem, child?"

"Jack's helping me." She was almost shouting. The priest had neither pulled closer nor had Hazel gone up to the car. She heard Jack coming from behind her. "Jack's always helping."

"Since when is that a sin, Father?" Jack laughed with the priest at his window. They spoke—as easy and as animated as they were in church, picking up where they left off—until Jack slapped the hood twice. The priest drove away, and Hazel walked back toward her car. She must have been in a daze. All she did was turn, and Jack was already there bent over the tire, legs butterflied out, feeling up under the chassis. Jack didn't know a thing about cars.

"Need anything?" she asked. "I have a flashlight in the back."

He laughed. She had not meant this to be a joke, but she understood. "Just get in the Jeep," he said. "We don't have all night." It was unforgivable how easily he said it.

"It's your fault I moved back," she said. "I hate this place." Then she turned and left him with it. Why not say it? That's what she thought sometimes. It wouldn't be so strange. They'd lived here together for years. Jack had been offered a position at a university in Michigan, and they had stood on the beach with the real estate agent and looked at the lake frozen into waves. When she lived in Cincinnati, he'd made arrangements to follow—a sabbatical, a leave of absence, something. How stupid to waste that time on her. She had nothing to offer him. And so she left for Miami before he could go through with it. But she'd heard things. The old story: just married to a sweet girl, a changed laugh, a new hairstyle. Aren't most marriages a cry for help? There are certain rights, privileges, Hazel took for granted in relationships both past and present, and no man had ever taught her otherwise. A man, once hers, remained hers.

Hazel rapped her knuckles on the Jeep's windshield. Theresa waved her in. As expected, Jack had not been difficult. A coffee, a beer. She'd apologized for her past behavior, took an interest. Hazel opened the back door. She tapped the snow out of her boots and adjusted her coat and thought of what else she could do to slow her entering into the Jeep. Jack had started attending conferences—everything could be covered with a conference—long weekends away, hangovers and erratic moods. Hazel did not care for Theresa. Though Theresa was only a few years younger than Hazel, Hazel still thought of her as a child—that was how she remembered her, sniveling.

The girl in the car seat was six and sleeping. Theresa had placed a blanket over the girl's head, which seemed both thoughtful and humane, as though she'd given her just enough ether.

"Why don't you sit up here? So I can see you."

"Oh, no," Hazel said. "Too much traffic on that side."

"I told Jack to stop. I was sure it was you."

"It was a beautiful program." There was a tone in Hazel's voice that she'd like to be rid of. Tight, manufactured.

"This one was Prancer. That's probably why she's out like a light—too much excitement."

"Of course you'd be there. I hadn't thought."

"The Christmas program is my favorite part of the year. Even when we were young. I was too nervous to be in it, but Tillie took me sometimes."

"I thought it was mandatory," Hazel said. Hazel was not meant to be a mother. She was not meant to speak with mothers.

"Tillie thought I was nervous. She would call the school and say I had the stomach flu—Spanish flu, she called it—but we would sometimes watch from the back. Even in high school."

"It's probably better to watch."

"I think so," Theresa said. She adjusted her head against its rest. It was a maternal gesture, content. All Hazel could see were shifting shadows and snow. "It's so beautiful out here," Theresa said. "It's such a beautiful night. It feels—well, it's almost religious, the way I feel. Like I should come out into the cold to pray every night. To be affected. But these are special circumstances." She reached her hand back for Hazel's knee and rubbed her mitten along Hazel's nylons.

"I wouldn't know," Hazel said.

"I thought Jack said you were religious. I mean, I thought I remembered that about you. Your mother too, of course. But things change. In the blink of an eye, you can turn out differently."

"He talks about me?"

"Does he? He thinks you came back because you ran out of places to go. He's worried you'll marry some guy from Shullsburg—that one we were all afraid of in high school."

"I don't know that guy."

"But you remember him, right? With the matches?" Theresa laughed. "And I'm sure he remembers you—who doesn't? No, I say, Hazel can go anywhere she likes, and since when is that a problem?"

"It's hard to catch my breath sometimes. I think I'm overwhelmed, but with what? I don't have anything left."

"Jack needs to give you a rest, that's all. Some things never change."

Jack had surprised her—he came over for a rare Saturday afternoon. Hazel's car keys were in her hand. She'd had plans—the kind of plans a single woman makes, coffee and maybe a movie with some friend so inconsequential to her, Hazel couldn't remember her name now. She'd skipped the coffee, no call. After, she'd rolled back onto her keys and hardly noticed until Jack pulled them out from under her and turned off the car alarm.

"Isn't it strange," she'd said to Jack.

"What's that?"

She'd been embarrassed.

"Yes?"

"Yes," Hazel had said. "Sometimes I think I might love you." Once, years back, she had sent him one hundred love haiku. It had been a joke. Some sorry student's work from when she tutored. She'd run a copy and signed it with love. But he had been so pleased with them that she hadn't had the heart to tell him. The haiku were probably in a shoebox somewhere in a closet Theresa would need a footstool to reach.

"Why wouldn't you? Is it because I'm married?"

"Theresa? No."

"You feel you can't trust me now. I was worried about that."

"Of course I can trust you. You're like a puppy. You're there, and then you're there."

Pillow talk, that was all she'd meant. She'd rose from his chest and tapped him on the nose. She'd laughed over his face and waited for him to roll her over and start the game all over again.

And so he had, but she could see it happening. Dog, puppy, pet. Pride, distraction—she'd never seen it in him before. Later, he pulled on his shorts and so on and left the room.

In the kitchen, he'd paced and opened the refrigerator, the cupboards. "You don't have any food in here," he'd said.

"I don't like to eat alone."

He'd pulled some old bread from its bag and warmed it in the oven. Butter, jam. They'd stood at the kitchen counter and ate it. That night, they'd gone down the street to a bar, some place they'd frequented at twenty, twenty-one. Beer flags hung from the ceiling. The place was empty except for a table of off-duty cops in the back. The bartender played country music on a boom box by the taps. Hazel and Jack got a pitcher. "I can't believe we're ending it in a bar," she said. Had she said it to beat him to it? At this age, were you supposed to say anything at all? She could have sworn she'd said the same thing years ago, sitting right there with her back to the window.

*

Someone had pulled over in front of Hazel's car, and he worked with Jack. He was tall and thin and pointed to many areas Jack had not yet visited.

"But why a bank teller?" Theresa asked. "I thought you'd be a—well, I don't know, a—"

"It just happened."

"That doesn't just happen. No offense."

Hazel watched the men jack up her car. They were putting on a show now, her car angled even further into the ditch. The red taillights blinked into the snow. It had been a long time since someone had done that, tried to win her with a gesture. Her father could not stand the foolishness. And Jack was only taunting her now. She decided she would call Smith when she got home. It was something she often did these days. He had moved when she left, some new job in Maryland. There had not been much for them in Miami. That was what she told herself when she thought about him: it was only the situation that had failed them.

"I have a fiancé in Miami, you know. Well, Maryland." Sometimes, not even she could tell whether she was lying.

"Miami. Don't you miss it tonight?"

"No. Miami's a joke."

Theresa laughed.

"You must have liked something," she said.

"The coffee was good." It had been their one luxury. Saturdays and Sundays spent at the café and never the beach. Dipping croissants and flipping through a copy of the *Times* that someone had left behind. Both she and Smith had felt like imposters there—the people who read the *Times* on Sundays, the people who could buy art. But they had indulged in the best coffee. The apartment was filled with the smell. "The dog would jump on the counter and lick our cups in the sink while we were at work."

"You had a dog." Theresa's voice was filled with wonder, as though someone had just told her a secret. It was only the snow. It made people feel that way in December. Religious. Theresa had been right to say so earlier.

Hazel said, "The smell of coffee always reminds me of the mall in Madison. You know the one specialty store they used to have? The whole walkway smelled like coffee—caramel and chestnuts."

"I never went to Madison until Jack. Tillie didn't drive much."

"We would go there every Christmas—the whole family. We kept a list all year with everything we needed that we could get on sale just then." It amazed Hazel now, that they could wait a year for a new belt or a toaster, how they would make do until then. She and Smith would run to the store if their pants even hinted at becoming baggy. Still, the two had looked run-down and thrown together most of the time they were together.

"Our coffee at the farm smelled nothing like it," Hazel said. "It was dishwater compared to this stuff."

The daughter woke and stretched her arms out toward the snow. The blanket fell to her waist. Theresa turned, and the girl called to her. She reached one arm toward Theresa and one toward the snow falling to her left—delighted. Jack was now in Hazel's car. The driver's side door was open, and he was calling back to the tall man, who was pushing. The tires spun until the car skidded and swerved onto the road, which was nearly deserted once again.

Theresa cheered.

In the mall, Hazel's parents would stand in the crowd with their shopping bags and their winter boots laced tightly, wondering if they would get a cup, if they dared to splurge. If it would be any good. "Why don't you just go in and get one?" Liz would say. In Hazel's memory, Liz is always sixteen and rushed, the voice of reason. But her family didn't drink the coffee, not once. They had known all the things they could do without, which was more than Hazel could hope to know.

Acknowledgments

For seeing something in this writing and deciding to do all the intricate and patient work of putting it out into the world, I'd like to thank Michelle Herman, Kristen Elias Rowley, Kelsey Hagarman, Eliza Smith, Ohio State's MFA Program in Creative Writing, and the Ohio State University Press.

I'm indebted to, and incredibly thankful for, the following:

The MFA program at Western Michigan University, including the Prague Summer Program, and particularly Jaimy Gordon, Richard Katrovas, Don Lee, Nancy Eimers, William Olson, and Gwen Tarbox, who always knows the next step. My colleagues, especially Rachel Swearingen, who knows how to come in with the save. Kellie Wells and Debra Marquart, for visiting, and Nick Dybek, who told me what an MFA was in the first place.

The Pod, that group of irreplaceable impossibles: Melinda Moustakis, Hilary Selznick, Kate Dernocoeur, Meghann Meeusen, and Kory Shrum.

The PhD program at the University of Cincinnati, where I was more fortunate than I can say to find Leah Stewart, Michael Griffith, and Chris Bachelder, and also the Taft Research Center, for granting me a fellowship while I was there. The talented friends and colleagues I gained during my years there, who have inspired and helped me, especially: Michelle Burke, Rachel Steiger-Meister, Heather Williams, Don Peteroy, Tessa Mellas, Liv Stratman, Becky Adnot-Haynes, Dietrik Vanderhill, Leah McCormack, Chris Koslowski, Julia Velasco Espejo, Brian Trapp, Marjorie Celona, Mark Manibusan, Suzanne Williams Wendell, David James Poissant, Joe and Catie Dargue, and Catherine O'Shea.

Chelsie Bryant, who always suggested I enter this contest. Patrick O'Keeffe, for offering a fellow farmer wisdom in the writing world. Nick Story, for being the most excellent first reader.

The faculty and friends I had at Augustana College—you opened a new and needed world. Emily Johnson, you would have found a better way to say all of this.

The Village of Potosi—teachers, coaches, friends, and all who contributed to making it a home where possibility thrived, especially the late Mary Fiorenza.

The many members of my urban family—too many to name—who have extended kindness to me as I wander, including Tyler Kieler, Daryl Osuch, and Joe Hartwich.

Jesse Nelman, who has been my partner-in-crime, the gale-force wind beneath my wings, for many years now, and Bouvier, who is, after all, a good dog.

My family, who I know I will never be able to properly thank. It is daunting to even begin. Eternal thanks to Dennis and Connie Zlabek for their endless support in this bizarre task of writing, and for giving me free reign on books at a young age. Jon, Michelle, Cassie, and Caitlin Zlabek, for the encouragement. Jennifer, Matt, Sam, and Grace George, for offering safe haven and more. Grace, for persistently asking how many books I have published—in its own way, it's fortifying. Sister, for putting up with your sister.

Note: Many stories in this collection, most particularly "Love Me, and the World Is Mine" and "Let the Rivers Clap Their Hands" utilize Midwestern news and lore. Sections of "Love Me" were inspired by the history of St. John's Mine in Potosi, Wisconsin, and a mysterious postcard I found in our family's documents. The lyrics that Tillie refers to come from a song of the same name, written by Dave Reed Jr. and Ernest R. Ball, and is often sung by barbershop quartets, though I know the song only because it was featured on said postcard. I wrote much of "Rivers" during the Flood of 2008, when it seemed the land and the people had reached the limits of endurance. In "Passing," the text *You have not come to something that can be touched, a blazing fire, and darkness, and gloom, and a tempest, and the sound of a trumpet and a voice whose words made the hearers beg that not another word be spoken to them* comes from Hebrews 12. Many stories here allude to Biblical figures or events—I am a regular reader of the book, and I'd like to extend my thanks in that mysterious direction, as well.

Finally, thank you to the following journals, their editors and readers, for originally publishing these stories and getting the ball rolling:

"Fennimore," *Ninth Letter.* University of Illinois at Urbana-Champaign. (Spring, 2018)

"Higgins," *Boulevard.* (Spring, 2017)

"Circumstances," *Quiddity: International Literary Journal and Public Radio Program.* (Spring, 2017)

"If There Is Need of Blessings," *The Kenyon Review,* Kenyon College, OH. (Jan/Feb, 2017)

"Hunting the Rut" (AWP Intro Award Winner), *Artful Dodge,* The College of Wooster, OH. (Summer, 2016)

"Love Me, and the World Is Mine," *The Literary Review,* Fairleigh Dickenson University, NJ. (Spring, 2014)

"So Very Nice," *Bayou,* University of New Orleans, LA. (Spring, 2014)

"Passing," *The Weekly Rumpus, The Rumpus.* (November 20, 2013)

"Let the Rivers Clap Their Hands," *TINGE,* Temple University, Philadelphia, PA. (Spring, 2011)

And to Ricochet Editions, for publishing *Let The Rivers Clap Their Hands,* a chapbook that includes the titular story, along with "Love Me, and the World Is Mine," in 2015.

THE JOURNAL NON/FICTION PRIZE
(formerly The Ohio State University Prize in Short Fiction)

When: Stories
Katherine Zlabek

Out of Step: A Memoir
Anthony Moll

Brief Interviews with the Romantic Past
Kathryn Nuernberger

Landfall: A Ring of Stories
Julie Hensley

Hibernate
Elizabeth Eslami

The Deer in the Mirror
Cary Holladay

How
Geoff Wyss

Little America
Diane Simmons

The Book of Right and Wrong
Matt Debenham

The Departure Lounge: Stories and a Novella
Paul Eggers

True Kin
Ric Jahna

Owner's Manual
Morgan McDermott

Mexico Is Missing: And Other Stories
J. David Stevens

Ordination
Scott A. Kaukonen

Little Men: Novellas and Stories
Gerald Shapiro

The Bones of Garbo
Trudy Lewis

The White Tattoo: A Collection of Short Stories
William J. Cobb

Come Back Irish
Wendy Rawlings

Throwing Knives
Molly Best Tinsley

Dating Miss Universe: Nine Stories
Steven Polansky

Radiance: Ten Stories
John J. Clayton

CPSIA information can be obtained
at www.ICGtesting.com
Printed in the USA
BVHW032350031019
560189BV00001B/3/P